Charm the dog, win the lady

Aaron got down on his haunches and scratched the dog behind the ears. "Hello, Fluffy. Well, the name fits. And you're a good girl, aren't you? You don't mean to be unruly, do you?"

Judy laughed, a pleasant, throaty laugh that sounded almost musical. "Oh, she likes you," she said as Fluffy began butting Aaron's hand with her wet nose. Another spontaneous leap brought the dog's front paws against his shoulders.

"Bad dog, Fluffy!" Judy said. "I'm really sor—"

Aaron held up his hand, traffic-cop style. "If you'd teach that little rapscallion some manners, you wouldn't have to apologize. And I'm volunteering."

"Volunteering?"

"To show you how to train her." *You're a genius,* he thought smugly. *From the ashes of disaster...*

Dear Reader:

The spirit of the Silhouette Romance Homecoming Celebration lives on as each month we bring you six books by continuing stars!

And we have a galaxy of stars planned for 1988. In the coming months, we're publishing romances by many of your favorite authors such as Annette Broadrick, Sondra Stanford and Brittany Young. Beginning in January, Debbie Macomber has written a trilogy designed to cure any midwinter blues. And that's not all—during the summer, Diana Palmer presents her most engaging heros and heroines in a trilogy that will be sure to capture your heart.

Your response to these authors and other authors of Silhouette Romances has served as a touchstone for us, and we're pleased to bring you more books with Silhouette's distinctive medley of charm, wit and—above all—romance.

I hope you enjoy this book and the many stories to come. Come home to romance—for always!

Sincerely,

Tara Hughes
Senior Editor
Silhouette Books

GLENDA SANDS

Treadmills and Pinwheels

Silhouette Romance

Published by Silhouette Books New York

America's Publisher of Contemporary Romance

SILHOUETTE BOOKS
300 E. 42nd St., New York, N.Y. 10017

Copyright © 1987 by Glenda Sands

ISBN: 0-373-08538-9

First Silhouette Books printing November 1987

America's Publisher of Contemporary Romance

Printed in the U.S.A.

Books by Glenda Sands

Silhouette Romance

The Mockingbird Suite #337
A Taste of Romance #389
Heart Shift #409
Tall, Dark and Handsome #434
Amended Dreams #447
Hero on Hold #477
Logan's Woman #496
The Things We Do for Love #514
Treadmills and Pinwheels #538

GLENDA SANDS's

feature-writing career led her to cow lots and campaign trails, chimney sweeps and cookie entrepreneurs before she, as she puts it, "stumbled onto the primrose path of fiction." A native Texan, Ms. Sands now lives in Florida with her husband and two children.

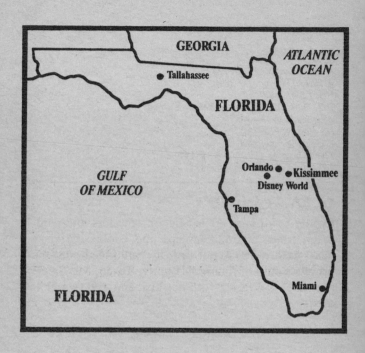

Chapter One

Seven stemmed glasses were lifted into the air above English bone china that reposed regally on a bed of off-white linen. "To our newest associate," said Trace Simpson, president of the Florida division of Butterfield Investments.

"To our newest associate," echoed the voices of Bob Borden, vice president for customer accounts and Jack Sawyer, vice president for accounting.

Glasses were raised and brought to lips. The vintage wine slid down J. Hollis Aaron's dry throat easily. *So nice to be welcomed in style,* he thought.

The cloud of tension enshrouding the group dissipated almost tangibly as everyone sat down. "So how does it feel to be on the Florida team?" Jack Sawyer said amiably from across the table.

Aaron flashed a charming smile. "Considering that it was twenty-two degrees and snowing when I left New York, Florida feels quite cozy."

"You'll get soft and spoiled like the rest of us," Sawyer predicted.

"Take my word for it, you'll love it," Beth Sawyer assured him. "You couldn't get me back up north on a bet. It's November, and we're still using the pool."

"It might take me a week or two to get used to it," Aaron said, drawing a round of polite laughter before everyone's attention was diverted to the romaine-and-mandarin-orange salad being served.

The entrées had been served before Virginia Simpson, seated on Aaron's left, said, "I just put the names Hollis and Aaron together. Are you Maxine Hollis's son?"

"You know my mother?" Aaron said, cocking an eyebrow.

"We were sorority sisters. I ran into her at the reunion just last summer. Trace, can you believe this? Your new vice president is almost family."

"I guess that comes under the heading of small world, doesn't it?" Simpson said.

"I can't believe it," Virginia said, resting a manicured hand on the top of Aaron's arm. "You're going to have to get Maxine down here soon so she and I can really catch up on the last thirty-odd years. Did she say your father was a plastic surgeon?"

"Orthopedic," Aaron said.

Virginia continued undaunted. "When I saw her in July, Maxine was all in a dither over an upcoming wedding. Does that mean your bride will be joining you soon?"

Aaron physically fought the frown forming on his lips. "I'm afraid that arrangement didn't work out."

Sympathy contorted the delicate features of Virginia's still-pretty face. "I'm so sorry to hear that," she said, pausing just in case he might volunteer some information about the broken engagement. When he didn't, she said,

"We'll just have to see to it you don't get too lonely here while you're getting settled."

Aaron could see the future predicted by the statement, the launch of his second career as a suitable extra man, a coup for any hostess. He would be invited to an endless string of dinner parties and asked to fill out numerous bridge tables and enliven countless cocktail parties. He flashed his best smile at Virginia Simpson. "I feel more at home already."

He'd heaved a giant sigh of relief on his way out of New York. It had been close this time, his narrow escape from the state of holy matrimony. He'd left behind a bitter ex-fiancée and brought with him a strong resolve never to get cornered again. After his suffocating experience with Melissa Aaron was ready to play the field, and he had a whole peninsula to play on. And now there was Virginia Simpson—his boss's wife, his mother's sorority sister—eager to launch him into the social swim. He couldn't have written a better scenario.

He wasn't expecting Mrs. Simpson to call so soon—on the first workday following the dinner welcoming him to the Florida office. She sounded hesitant, almost shy, quite different from the confident woman he'd perceived her to be. "I was wondering—" she hesitated, and the timbre of her voice changed "—could you possibly meet me for lunch today, Aaron?"

Aaron eyed the stack of file folders on his desk, all filled with information he needed to learn backward and forward before he could get started on his new job. He'd planned on reading through lunch, maybe calling somewhere to have a sandwich delivered.

"It's very important," Mrs. Simpson said, sensing his ambivalence.

She was his boss's wife. It would be career and social suicide to offend her, and downright stupid. "Certainly, Mrs. Simpson."

"Virginia," she corrected, sounding disproportionately relieved. "There's a restaurant—Monty's—a few blocks north of the office. They have a soup-and-salad buffet. Shall we meet at eleven to beat the crowd?"

"That sounds fine."

"Oh, Aaron..."

"Yes?"

"I'd appreciate...please don't...you'll understand later, but please don't mention that we're meeting to anyone."

Apprehension prickled Aaron's scalp. *What the hell was going on here?* "Sure. Of course, Mrs....Virginia."

The restaurant's ambience was cozy and the food was above average, but Aaron was too preoccupied to enjoy either. He'd welcomed Virginia Simpson's maternal interest in him, but he wasn't sure what this lunch was all about. Aaron's vast experience with women had never included clandestine rendezvous with other men's wives, and such a liaison was not in his current plans, especially with a woman who had gone to college with his mother. If Virginia Simpson had love in the afternoon on her mind, he was in one hell of a mess, one that would require some fancy footwork to dance his way out of.

A roving waitress cleared away their plates and poured coffee, and Aaron and Virginia both declined a selection from the dessert cart. Virginia folded her napkin neatly, laid it on the table in front of her and sighed languidly. Aaron drew in a fortifying lungful of air and released it slowly.

"I guess you're wondering why I asked you here," she said. Her shoulders drooped wearily as she sighed again. "That sounds like a line from a British drawing-room mystery, doesn't it?" Aaron shifted uncomfortably in his seat. "I talked to your mother yesterday," Virginia said.

"Oh?"

"She says you weren't exactly distraught over your broken engagement."

"My mother's irritated because she doesn't have any grandchildren. She talks too much."

"You've got to understand that I wasn't prying," Virginia continued. "I just wanted to find out if you were recovering from a shattering experience. Since you're not..." Again the tone of her voice changed abruptly. "I have a problem, Aaron. I'm desperate, and I think you could help me."

Aaron had a gut instinct that Virginia's "problem" meant trouble. "Mrs. Simp—"

"Virginia," she corrected. "Please. Hear me out before you say no." Aaron sat perfectly still. "I have a son—" she hesitated "—actually I have two sons and a daughter, but it's my baby I'm concerned about. He's nineteen."

Aaron fought the impulse to roll his eyes in exasperation as he waited for her to continue. "Gregory's a good kid, Aaron, he really is, and bright. He's a freshman at Rollins College. But he's become involved... There's a girl. No, I take that back. It's not a girl, it's a woman, and that's why I'm so upset." Her hand crossed the narrow table to clamp over Aaron's. "You're the only person who could help me."

Aaron was extremely uncomfortable. Whatever Virginia Simpson wanted from him, he wanted no part of it. He shook his head slowly. "I don't know what you think I could do for you, but I'm sure I couldn't—"

"Oh, but you could, Aaron. And you're the only person who can. You haven't found a place to live yet, have you?"

"No," he admitted cautiously.

"Butterfield Investments holds a large interest in the condominium complex where my son is living. Trace and I bought a couple of units, which is why Gregory is living there. The girl—woman—he's involved with owns a unit there, too. I guess that's where they met. At least I don't think it's been going on more than a couple of months, and he just moved there in September to start school."

She took a deep breath and a long sip of coffee. "This woman is twenty-six years old, Aaron."

"So?"

Virginia sniffed exasperatedly. "What do you suppose she sees in a nineteen-year-old boy?"

"Maybe she goes for younger men."

"She's a bloodsucker," Virginia said. "She's seen his fancy car and done some homework and found out we live on an acre and a half of lakefront property and thinks she's latching on to a fortune."

"Don't you think you might be overre—"

"I'm a mother," Virginia snapped. "Mothers have an instinct. She's already got him slinking around behind my back. I wouldn't even have found out about the entire affair if Stan over at the bank hadn't called me about the four hundred dollars—"

"Start at the beginning, Virginia. What four hundred dollars?"

"The four-hundred-dollar share loan Gregory took out against his school fund to buy this little . . . strumpet a birthday present." Virginia's frustration and concern were genuine. "He has a credit card. Why didn't he use it? I'll tell you, because he didn't want a record of whatever it is he bought crossing his father's desk or mine.'' A funny cracking sound rose from her throat.

Oh, Lord, thought Aaron. *Please don't let her cry.* Spreading his hands in the air in a gesture of futility, Aaron said, ''Virginia, may I speak frankly with you?''

''Certainly.''

''You may be a mother, but I'm a mother's son, and if you don't mind a word of advice I'd say you're probably overreacting to the entire situation. And even if you're not, if you start meddling in your son's life, he's going to resent it. If he senses your resistance to this relationship, he's going to cling to this girl just to spite you. Chances are if you leave him alone he'll lose interest in her.''

''If it were a *girl* I'd do just that, but we're dealing with a *woman* here. What could she possibly want with a nineteen-year-old boy if she's not trying to coerce him into marriage?''

''Some women like younger men. It could be purely physical.''

''Gregory's a nice-looking young man, but he's still a kid, all arms and legs. No, Aaron, she's after my son, and I can't just sit idly by and let him get devoured by a barracuda. You've got to help me save him.''

Aaron unconsciously ran a finger between his neck and the collar that seemed to be shrinking as Mrs. Simpson edged closer to hysteria. ''What is it you think I can do?''

''You can move into one of our condos there. We'd write you a six-month lease with an option to buy it if you like it.''

''I still don't see—''

''I want you to meet this girl, see what the situation is and distract her.''

''*Distract* her?''

"Turn on that charm of yours. Why would this woman want a boy when she could have a man?"

Exasperated, Aaron slapped his hand on the table. "Has it occurred to you that Gregory and this girl might actually care for each other?"

"My son is nineteen years old, and he's in his first year of college. A liaison with a twenty-six-year-old woman could only hurt him at this point. Believe me, if he were a few years older and not so naive, if this girl were only closer to his age, I'd let him sink or swim."

"Can't you try talking to him?"

"He'd only balk, as you pointed out. At this point he doesn't know I know about this woman, and it's just as well he never finds out."

"And you don't think he's going to get suspicious when one of the men from his father's firm shows up and starts wooing this girl away?"

"He's likely to get mad as hell at you for taking his girl away, but he's not going to connect you with me. It's only natural that you would look through the Butterfield Investments projects when you start house-hunting."

"I guess you've talked this little arrangement over with my mother," Aaron said, frowning.

Virginia shrugged innocently. "I might have mentioned it. And of course Maxine was in complete agreement with me that something has to be done."

"Of course," Aaron said, with the stone weight of entrapment sinking in his middle. The only prospect worse than having his new boss's wife angry with him was the even more abominable prospect of some nagging via long-distance phone calls from his mother.

Virginia seemed to recognize a fait accompli when she saw one. With a hefty sigh of relief, she said, "The woman's name is Judy Harte. It shouldn't be difficult for a man with your... savoir faire to engineer a meeting in a small condominium complex.''

Chapter Two

Sooner or later, Aaron thought, the lady had to check her mail. It was the third evening he'd hung around the bank of mailboxes in his quest to meet Judy Harte. If the lady didn't show tonight, he'd have to resort to knocking on her door and asking to borrow a cup of sugar. It was corny, but he'd tried it once, and accompanied by "Actually I can't cook, but I saw you in the parking garage and wanted to meet you," it had worked.

So far he had not caught even the briefest glimpse of the elusive Ms. Harte, and meeting her was the last thing he *wanted* to do. What he would have liked to do was forget he'd ever heard the name Judy Harte. What she and Gregory did behind closed doors mattered not one whit to him, and the idea of wooing a woman sight unseen to break up what might be a beautiful relationship left a bitter taste in his mouth.

Face it, you're between a rock and a hard place, old man, he thought morosely, indulging in the luxury of self-pity, *and all because your mother wants grandbabies while she's young enough to rock them*. She'd willed this on him; he could feel it. Oh, she hadn't come up with the specifics; she'd just directed a barrage of negative vibes due south to rain disaster on him in retribution for his broken engagement. And Virginia Simpson had picked them up with that radar mothers have. The weaker sex, indeed! With forces like his mother and Virginia Simpson loose in the world, why would anyone waste time worrying about nuclear weapons?

A tall redhead in a green linen suit entered the walkway from the parking lot with a set of keys in her hand. Aaron sauntered nonchalantly to the bank of mailboxes to see if she was opening the right box.

False alarm—not only did she go to the wrong box, Aaron noticed the flash of a diamond wedding set on her left ring finger. Fortune hunters, he thought uncharitably, rarely wear wedding bands until after they've snared their game.

Another ten minutes crept by, and Judy Harte's mailbox remained abysmally unattended. Feeling hunger pains, Aaron decided to give it up for the day before someone noticed him loitering and became suspicious. *Don't worry, everyone. I'm not a pervert. I'm just a poor schnook on a spy-and-distract mission for my mom's old sorority sister.*

He had thought about Judy Harte enough for one evening. On the way to his condo he concentrated instead on his own problem, hunger, and the decision of which local restaurant he would choose to entrust the task of titillating his taste buds to. From the corner of his eye he registered the sight of a woman walking a dog, or rather of a woman being pulled along by an unwieldy overgrown puppy on a nearby sidewalk.

A pang of homesickness, the first one since he'd moved, swept through him as he thought of the setters he and his father had raised. He was going to miss being able to drive out to the estate on Sunday afternoons and take the dogs for a romp. He'd only made it home once a month or so, but thinking of those visits brought vivid memories and remembered sensations. He could almost smell the rye bread his mother would bake for him. His mother didn't enjoy cooking, and making the rye bread he loved was her special method of pampering him. One loaf would be sliced, still warm, with dinner; the other would be sent back to the city with him, wrapped in vague echoes of his mother's disappointment over his solitary life-style—a life-style that was depriving her of what she perceived to be the one consolation of advancing age: grandchildren.

"Fluffy! No-o-o!" The sharp, desperate cry drew him back to the present just as two substantial sand-encrusted paws landed against his right thigh and a slobbery tongue made contact with his hand.

Immediately the girl with the dog wrapped her arm around the dog's chest and tugged it away from him. "Bad doggie!" she scolded, slipping her hand through the dog's collar. "I'm sorry. She's a little rambunctious."

Reflexively her free hand flew up to dust the sandy paw prints from his pants in a futile effort to undo the damage her pet had wrought. Aaron, caught off guard, had no way of telling whether she sensed his immediate reaction to her touch on his thigh or whether she just suddenly became aware of the impropriety of brushing the sand from a strange man's trousers, but she jerked her hand away abruptly.

"I'm sorry about your pants," she said clumsily. "I'll wash them for you."

"They're not washable," Aaron said, and he regretted the harshness of his tone of voice when he saw the distress in the liquid green of her eyes. She was shorter than average, with full breasts and hips and a trim waist, and her curly, chin-length brown hair was as unruly as her mutt's, but utterly feminine.

"I'll pay for the dry cleaning, then," she said. She was wearing a pair of faded denim shorts and an equally faded T-shirt with a picture of an apple on it under the slogan Teachers Are a Class Act.

Shaking his head, he said, "No need, really. They were ready to go to the cleaners anyway."

The dog made a sudden lurch and, escaping the girl's clasp, planted his paws against Aaron's left thigh and, tail wagging fiercely, directed eyes hidden behind a riot of hair toward Aaron's face. Aaron moved his foot forward and pressed it down over the dog's hind paw. The dog yipped, dropped into a standing position and tilted her head to one side quizzically.

There was nothing quizzical in the girl's expression. It was pure vehemence as she glared at him. "You didn't have to hurt her. She's just a dumb an—"

"I didn't hurt her," Aaron said. "I merely surprised her. It's a standard training procedure for dogs that jump on people. You saw how quickly she responded."

"And heard how loudly she cried."

"I did *not* hurt her!" Aaron repeated, exasperated at being cast in the role of villain. "It was just a gentle pinch to get her attention. If you're going to own a dog, you should train it properly instead of letting it drag you all over the sidewalk and jump on people. Otherwise, you *and* your dog are going to wind up frustrated and unhappy."

Color rose high in the girl's cheeks, and fury flashed in the green of her eyes. "I told you I was sorry for your inconvenience. Look, my name is Judy Harte and I live in 22-B, and if you'll bring me the receipt for having your pants cleaned I'll reimburse you. But if you expect me to stand here and listen to lectures on how to raise my dog, or grovel at your feet apologizing because a puppy is a little bit rambunctious, then you're going to be sorely disappointed."

Judy Harte. Aaron stood there staring at her, unable to believe that this fuzzy-headed runt of a girl-next-door could be the mercenary vamp troubling Virginia Simpson's sleep. Nevertheless, she had clearly said her name was Judy Harte, and Aaron realized he had to act fast to salvage the situation. "Whoa! Peace!" he said, raising his hand in the air.

Judy regarded him with cautious interest, and he continued. "We seem to have gotten off on the wrong foot here, and if we're going to be neighbors I'd rather have a friend than an enemy. How about a truce?"

He answered the skeptical tilt of her eyebrow with his most charming smile. "I could start by getting to know your dog. What's her name again?"

"Fluffy," Judy said.

Charm the dog, win the lady. Aaron got down on his haunches and scratched the dog behind the ears. "Hello, Fluffy. Well, the name fits. And you're a good girl, aren't you? Yeah. You don't mean to be unruly, do you? No. You just like to be petted. What breed is she?"

"She's a cross between a mutt and an undetermined fence-jumper," Judy said, kneeling so that she was on the same level as Aaron.

"Are you sure?" Aaron said. "There's something familiar about her features and her coat...."

Judy laughed, a pleasant, throaty laugh that sounded almost musical. "That's because she's got so many breeds in her. Oh, she likes you," she said as Fluffy began butting Aaron's hand with a wet nose. Another spontaneous leap brought the dog's front paws against his shoulder blades, and Aaron went tumbling backward.

He muttered an unintelligible obscenity as his backside landed ignobly on the concrete and a pink tongue applied wet affection in the vicinity of his nose.

"Bad dog, Fluffy!" Judy said, tugging at the dog's collar to wrest him off his prey.

So here I am, flat on my behind being kissed by a love-starved mongrel while a femme fatale in a faded T-shirt tries to rescue me, he thought. *Thank you, Mom, Mrs. Simpson.* Wondering fleetingly if there were any monasteries in Florida, he got up and brushed the dust from the seat of his pants.

"I'm really sor—"

He held up a hand, traffic-cop-style. "If you'd teach that little rapscallion some manners, you wouldn't have to go around apologizing for her. And I'm not lecturing, I'm volunteering."

"Volunteering?"

"To show you how to train her." *You're a genius, J. Hollis,* he thought smugly. *A positive genius. From the ashes of disaster...* Before she could protest, he said, "You've got a nice dog with a discipline problem, and I've trained a lot of dogs. What kind of friend would I be if I didn't give you the benefit of my experience?"

Judy stared down at the dog. A peculiar silence stretched between them while he waited for her to respond. "I'm not sure I want to train her," she said finally, softly. Then, as though she understood that he wouldn't understand, she looked at Aaron. "She's a dog. That's all I want her to be."

All she wants her dog to be is a dog? The girl was a certifiable dingdong. How was he supposed to charm this girl away from young Gregory when he wasn't even sure he could communicate with her?

"She's a good-size puppy now, but she's going to be a *big* dog," he said, forsaking charm in one final stab at logic. "If you can't control her now, how are you going to handle her when she's full-grown?"

Impatient, Fluffy jumped up to get Judy's attention. Her front paws landed on Judy's midriff, forcing her to do some fancy footwork to regain her balance. Judy sighed in exasperation while petting the dog with long, loving strokes from neck to shoulder blade. "I guess she *could* use a little canine etiquette." With all the joy and enthusiasm of a terminally ill patient asking the doctor how much longer she had to live, she looked up at Aaron and said, "What do I do first?"

"Well, unless you want Fluffy propping her feet on you like that, you can start by not rewarding her behavior."

She dropped her hands to her side. "Okay."

"Now tell her to get down. Just say 'Down' very firmly and pinch her paw with your foot."

"I can't do that."

"Then just say 'Down' and push down on her chest with both hands." He nodded approval when she followed his instructions. "Now do that every time she jumps up. Consistency is the key."

"She looks sad," Judy said.

"Not nearly as sad as you do," Aaron observed. "Why don't you praise her now that she's not—" He stopped in midsentence as Fluffy's front paws landed on his thighs.

The expression on Judy's face was far too smug as she raised her eyebrows and shrugged at the dog's behavior as if to say "I told you so."

Aaron frowned and said, "Down!" as he pushed on the dog's chest. For a few seconds his gaze and Fluffy's locked in mutual challenge, but the dog finally seemed to sense Aaron's authority and did not jump up again. Aaron leaned over and petted her behind the ears. Eyes closed, a beatific expression on her face, Fluffy cocked her head toward his stroking fingers.

Aaron did not miss the rather petulant pout playing at Judy's mouth as she observed the dog's response to his attention. Nor did he fail to notice that she had a nice mouth, with full, sensuous lips. Maybe this little favor he was doing for Mrs. Simpson wasn't going to be as repugnant as he'd anticipated.

Congratulations, old boy, on rejoining the human race. After a three-month fast, it's time you started noticing women again. He'd been celibate—emotionally as well as physically—since the debacle with Melissa.

Maybe the change of location was working.

"Why don't you try walking her now?" he said. "She's got to learn to heel."

She smiled unexpectedly. "Life is simple for you, isn't it?"

"I don't know what you mean."

"You're so sure of everything." She parodied him: " 'She's got to learn to heel.' "

He laughed softly. "If she doesn't learn to heel, you're going to wind up with a dislocated shoulder. That's simple logic. Now choke down on that leash. Don't give her but a few inches lead so you can control her."

"Like this?"

"That's good, but put her on the other side. Always on the left."

Judy shifted the leash from one hand to the other. "Always on the left?"

"Standard operating procedure."

Aaron heard the tincture of sarcasm in her voice as she said, "We certainly wouldn't want to deviate from standard operating procedure." She cocked her head at him haughtily. "Where to?"

He lifted his shoulders to show his open-mindedness and suggested, "Once around the courtyard?"

She nodded and started walking. He fell into step beside her. "Keep her right beside you. You're in control, remember."

"I'm not so sure of that," she said. "The last time I noticed, you were."

Aaron wondered how they'd gotten into this adversarial relationship and why he couldn't manage to pull out of it. He could hear the challenge in everything she said to him, the muted hostility in his own remarks, yet he seemed incapable of breaking the bait-and-snap cycle. "She's your dog," he said. "You have to work her. Say 'Heel' firmly and pull her back when she tries to take off like that." *Snap!*

"Heel!" Judy said, yanking on the leash. To Aaron: "I suspect you are used to being in control and you enjoy it." *Bait.*

Snap! "I'm not rigid, if that's what you mean."

"Rigidity is like beauty or pain. It's relative and subjective. Heel, Fluffy."

"You should get a metal choke collar. When dogs feel the pinch, they catch on a lot quicker."

"Choke collars are barbaric." *Bait.*

"They don't hurt the dog if you use them properly." *Snap!*

"I can't think of anything more *improper* than putting a device intended to choke an animal on a pet I'm supposed to love and care for."

This time he did the baiting. "Now who's rigid?"

"I'm rigid about not being rigid."

It was irrefutable. There simply was nothing Aaron could say to argue with the point she'd made. Heaven help Gregory Simpson if he was genuinely smitten with this girl. She probably had nineteen-year-olds for lunch!

They reached the first junction of sidewalks, turned and walked toward the next corner. "She's doing very nicely," Aaron said.

"She's an intelligent dog," Judy said, "even though she's a mutt."

"A lot of mutts are intelligent."

"I got the impression you'd much prefer her to be a registered something-or-other." *Bait.*

"What difference could it make to me whether she's a mutt or a national grand champion?" *Snap!*

"Why indeed?" Judy mumbled under her breath.

They turned the second corner. "Do you really teach school?" he said, remembering the slogan on her shirt.

"Do you really wear dry-cleanable-only clothes in Florida?"

Aaron stopped in midstep. "Did I miss something—like the half of this conversation that makes sense?"

Judy stopped, turned and regarded him interestedly.

"I asked if you taught school," Aaron continued, "and you asked if I wear dry-cleanable-only clothes in Florida. I don't see the connection."

"Heel!" Judy instructed Fluffy, and began walking again. Aaron lengthened his stride to catch up. "Yes, I teach school," she said. "And it's obvious you wear dry-cleanable-only clothes. I'd say we both know as much as we need to know about each other."

She stopped and planted her right hand on her hip. "Look, everything I wear to work is washable. Quite frankly, I've never met anyone who worked in dry-cleanables who had a lot of respect for what I do. And, to be perfectly blunt, I probably wouldn't have a lot of respect for what you do, either. What is it? Law? Banking?"

"Investments."

"Ah, yes. There is a definite aura of Wall Street about you." *Bait.*

"You say that as though Wall Street were a sewer." *Snap!*

Judy's silence was quite expressive.

Exasperated, Aaron said, "I've only been here two weeks. Give me a chance to get acclimated." To Fluffy, who had suddenly decided she needed some attention and had leaped on his thigh again, he growled, "Down!"

"Heel!" Judy said, and she took off with a rapid gait.

With his longer legs, Aaron caught up easily as they turned another corner. "You've got a big chip on your shoulder, did you know that?"

"I'm just a realist. The fact is, we could spend a lot of time getting to know one another, but the more we learned the more we'd realize we have very little in common."

Aaron, 32, was shot down by the sharp tongue of a feisty schoolteacher. He is survived by his mother, who wanted grandchildren, three bitter ex-fiancées and Virginia Simpson, who remains concerned about her nineteen-year-old son, Gregory, believed to be emotionally involved with the alleged perpetrator. Enough! thought Aaron. He was going to do the most sensible thing under the circumstances: he was going to call Virginia Simpson and tell her he'd attempted to court this Judy Harte and struck out. The apology and admission of failure would be humbling, but he'd be off the hook.

Like hell he was going to call Virginia Simpson and admit this little dynamo had gotten the better of him! He'd charmed college professors, advertising executives, corporate attorneys and a prominent Manhattan pediatrician. He'd be damned if a sawed-off schoolteacher with a tongue that dripped carbolic acid was going to send him back to his new boss's wife with his ears drooping and his tail between his legs. Old love-'em-and-leave-'em J. Hollis Aaron wasn't through with Judy Harte yet.

"What do you teach?" he asked.

"Take a guess."

Aaron imagined her surrounded by low tables, crayons and construction paper. "Kindergarten?"

She laughed, and he felt slightly scorched. "Sixth-grade science," she said.

"Science?"

"A few of us women have been able to grasp the concepts of gravity and centrifugal force. Some of us teach science."

"I wasn't casting chauvinistic aspersions. I was just surprised. Why sixth grade?"

"Any younger and I couldn't dig deep enough into the science."

"Why not high school, then?"

"My students would be taller than me."

"The sixth-graders aren't?"

She answered his smile with her own. With her full lips and large, even teeth, it was an attractive smile. "They haven't had all the curiosity bred out of them yet in sixth grade. By the time they reach high-school physics, they're too worried about getting into college to get excited over the actual learning."

"Do I hear a little criticism of the system in that remark?"

"No system's perfect. Certainly not the educational system. Just because we're a part of it doesn't mean we can't see the flaws. We have to see them, otherwise how can we correct them?"

"I'll bet you're good at pointing them out," he said wryly.

"I like to think I do as much as one human being can to correct the ones within my limited realm of operation." She stopped. "Well, we're back where we started. Fluffy's done well, hasn't she?"

"Exceptionally," he said, bending over to pet the dog. "And so did you."

"I'm a quick learner," she said, but an edge of bitterness seeped through her attempt at humor. Abruptly she tugged at Fluffy's leash, pulling the dog out of Aaron's reach. "Fluffy and I have to get home."

"I was just going to dinner," he said. "Why don't you go with me?"

"I'm not dressed," she said, looking down at her tattered knockabout clothing.

"I've got to change before I go anywhere. We could leave in half an hour or so."

Tightening Fluffy's lead, Judy started up the sidewalk. Then, from several yards ahead, she called over her shoulder, "I've got papers to grade, but thank you anyway."

"That's no way to treat a new friend, making him eat alone," he said, trailing after her. He seemed to be constantly chasing this woman—literally chasing her.

"I don't even know your name," she said.

"J. Hollis Aaron."

"Is that Jay, as in three letters like the bird, or *J* period, an initial?"

"*J* period."

"What does it stand for?"

"It doesn't matter."

"Of course it matters. It's your name."

He shrugged. "It doesn't matter because everyone calls me Aaron."

"If it didn't matter, you wouldn't use it to make your name sound important." Quickening her stride, she scurried ahead of him again.

"I don't use it to make my name sound important, dammit! It's part of my name," he told the back of her head.

"Then it matters," she called over her shoulder.

He stopped. What did she mean? For the life of him, he couldn't decide whether she was ridiculing him or flirting with him.

Chapter Three

You've got to teach this mutt some manners," Gregory Simpson told Judy, laughing as Fluffy's wet nose nuzzled his cheek.

"I was told that just recently," Judy said, remembering the episode with J. Hollis Aaron the previous afternoon. For an encounter—a brief interlude without beginning or destination—it had been rather stimulating. Too bad such gorgeous packaging had to be wasted on a Treadmill Clone like J. Hollis Aaron. Even his name was stuck on that treadmill, not allowed to be Jonathan or Joe or Jerry like one of the masses, but reduced instead to an initial to preface a highfalutin moniker that looked good on cream-colored linen-weave calling cards and company letterheads: *J. Hollis Aaron, Consummate Executive. Office hours: Nine to five. Destination: Success. Ambition: Terminal. Occupation: Treadmill Rat, genus Wall Street.*

Gregory was sitting Indian-style on the floor using the coffee table as a desk, and Fluffy bowled him over sideways with an unexpected lunge, then pinned him to the floor by placing her front paws on his chest and her muzzle in his face. "I wouldn't mind this if she had a cask of brandy on her collar," he said, laughing as he dodged the dog's flitting tongue.

"You're too young for brandy," Judy said. "She'd get arrested for contributing to your delinquency."

"How about calling her off, then?"

"Not until you promise to memorize that equation before you go to class on Friday."

"Oh, Jeez, Judy, have a heart. Damn, Fluffy, stop that, that tickles! Ju-dy, do something with your hound."

But it was the doorbell that rescued him, because Fluffy trailed after Judy as she answered the door. A smile at Fluffy's antics was still playing at the corners of Judy's mouth, and it lingered there even as surprise at seeing J. Hollis Aaron registered on her face. "J. Hollis," she said. It was less a greeting than an affirmation.

"Aaron," he corrected, stepping inside without waiting for an invitation.

Just come right on in, make yourself at home, Judy thought snidely.

Aaron thrust a brown grocery bag in her direction. "I was at the market and remembered a mutual friend."

Judy pulled a small box from the bag. "Doggie Delights?" she read incredulously.

Aaron had knelt to pet Fluffy, who was sniffing his feet. "Glad to see she's at the door protecting you."

"From wolves?" Judy asked wryly.

"Are you worried about wolves?" he asked, smiling fetchingly.

"Not *Canis lupus*," Judy said. "*They* have four legs."

Doggie biscuits! But then, why should that surprise her? She should have known that his attempt at seduction would be creative. He'd be persistent, too, especially when she resisted. Losing a challenge is not in the scheme of things for Wall Street Treadmill Clones. "Come on in," she said. "I'll open these for Fluffy."

"I thought we might take her out for another training session," he said, following Judy past the bookshelves that separated the entry hall from the living area. Gregory was just standing up, dusting the carpet lint from the seat of his corduroy jeans with his hands.

It had to be Gregory Simpson, Aaron thought, recognizing the pleasant combination of Virginia Simpson's fair skin and high cheekbones and a youthful version of Trace Simpson's wide jaw. Virginia had described him as all arms and legs, and indeed he was, but he was tall, too—well over six feet—and the result was an Ichabod Crane effect. He smiled self-consciously and nodded a greeting as Judy and Aaron came into sight.

"I'm not...interrupting anything, am I?" Aaron asked. The expression in his eyes as he looked at Judy and the beat of hesitation impregnated the question with innuendo.

Judy's eyes narrowed menacingly as she said, "J. Hollis Aaron, meet another neighbor. Gregory Simpson, meet J. Hollis Aaron. *J* the initial, not Jay like the bird."

"Just plain Aaron," Aaron said, shaking hands.

"Like a television tough guy," Judy said.

Aaron bristled at the barb and sent a scowl in her direction.

Judy shrugged. *"Magnum, Hunter, Kojak, Starsky and Hutch—"*

Pointedly ignoring her, Aaron looked down at the coffee table, where a notebook lay open in the midst of several textbooks. "Studying?"

"Judy's been helping me with physics," Gregory said.

"Gregory's a student at Rollins College."

"We'd given up on physics for the day and were trying to decide what kind of pizza to order when Fluffy decided it was time to play," Gregory said, picking up a pizza coupon that was lying on his notebook. "We've got the choices narrowed down to pepperoni-and-mushroom or supreme."

"Go for it," Aaron advised, "Get the supreme and have them hold the anchovies."

"The voice of decision," Judy said, with thinly veiled sarcasm. "So nice to have a man around to take charge." *And if you're not careful, he'll be taking charge of you,* she told herself. He was casually dressed today, but still shockingly handsome. "Shall I make the call, or do you want to?" she asked Gregory.

"I will," Gregory said, dropping into the overstuffed chair positioned perpendicular to the couch and referring to the coupon for the number as he used the desk phone on the end table.

Aaron was about to sit down on the couch when he noticed the display of pinwheels next to the wall. There were dozens of them, all colors, sizes and designs, their sticks mounted in holes drilled into special wooden shelves. Instead of sitting down, he walked to the wall to get a closer look at them and was studying one made of intricate lace foil when suddenly a current of air sent the entire lot into action. Turning, he discovered that Judy had switched on a small fan. She smiled at him. "Pretty, aren't they?"

"I never knew there were so many types."

"You wouldn't notice unless you were a connoisseur."

"And you obviously are a connoisseur."

She grew quiet suddenly, staring wistfully at the turning pinwheels. When she spoke, her voice was serious and low. "There was a time when I didn't notice that pinwheels could be beautiful.'' A bittersweet smile touched her lips.

There was a softness about her features as she watched the colorful wheels turning, and Aaron wondered at the fact that he had not noticed before that she was pretty in an exotic way. Perhaps, he thought wryly, he'd been too busy parrying her challenges to notice.

As quickly as it had come over her, the mellow mood dissolved. ''I use them in the classroom to illustrate wind power when we have the section on alternate power sources. Each of my students has to make one.''

''You're a good teacher, aren't you?'' he said.

Judy started to reply, but was pre-empted by a testimonial from Gregory. ''She's a great teacher. I'd be flunking if she weren't spoon-feeding me the technical details.'' Abruptly directing his attention to the telephone receiver, he said, ''Yes. I'd like to order two large pizzas....''

Aaron cocked an eyebrow at Judy. ''You were about to say?''

Her green eyes met his. ''That I don't know if I'm a good teacher. I like to think I am because I love teaching, and enthusiasm has to count for something.''

''We don't want it delivered, do we?'' Gregory said.

''It would take hours and get here soggy,'' Judy said.

''We'll pick it up,'' Gregory said into the telephone. Seconds later he hung up the receiver and announced, ''It'll be ready in twenty minutes.''

''That should give us just about enough time to take Fluffy on a training hike before you leave,'' Aaron said. Forestalling the protest forming on Judy's mouth, he added, ''You have to be consistent if you expect to make any progress.''

"Gregory and I will have to leave in ten minutes," she said, "and I was going to toss a salad, so there's not enough time to walk the dog, too."

"It doesn't take but one to pick up a pizza—Gregory, why don't you go, and then Judy and I can walk the dog and she'll still have time to toss a salad."

For a few seconds petulance hardened the lines of Gregory's mouth when he realized he was being manipulated, but then he accepted the fact. "Sure. Okay. I could get the pizza."

"But it's not fair to ask Gregory—" Judy said.

"It's all right," Gregory said. "I don't mind, really. And Lord knows she needs some training."

"Everything's settled then," Aaron said. "Right, Judy?"

"Oh, everything's just peachy-keen," she said flatly.

Gregory began closing and stacking his books. "I, uh, think I'll take my books over to my place before I go after the pizza." He grinned. "I don't want to be reminded of physics over dinner." At the door he said, "Oh, Judy, can I talk to you a minute?" He obviously intended it to sound casual and spontaneous, but it sounded rather grave.

Judy's eyes, swimming with hostility, met Aaron's. "Certainly," she told Gregory, and stepped outside with him. When she returned she was ready to do battle. Arms akimbo, she glowered at Aaron. "That was a rude, rotten thing to do."

Aaron, who was seated on the couch with Fluffy's chin propped up on his thigh, did not break the rhythm of the long, loving strokes his hands were delivering to her head. "What was?"

"Don't you play innocent with me. You're not going to pull the wool over my eyes. You deliberately humiliated Gregory, sending him off like some errand boy."

Oh, ho! thought Aaron. *The plot thickens. She's defending him.* "It made sense for him to go. Otherwise you weren't going to have time to work with Fluffy."

"You pompous nincompoop! Don't pretend it was Fluffy you had in mind when you came barging in here uninvited."

Very gently Aaron lifted the dog's chin off his leg and stood up. "If I didn't know better, I'd think you were accusing me of having ulterior motives for being here!"

"Where in the world would I get a ridiculous idea like that?" she said sarcastically.

Shrugging, Aaron said, "Beats the hell out of me. I certainly wouldn't want you to get the impression I'm *interested* in you, especially when you obviously already have a boyfriend."

"Gregory's not my boyfriend," she said. Then, realizing that she was *accounting* to this man, she jerked the dog's leash from the hook in the hall closet and added, "Not that it's any business of yours. Here, Fluffy, come on, girl."

At the door Aaron stepped beside her, closer, she thought, than was necessary, while she snapped the leash on Fluffy's collar. "Choke up on the line now, from the very beginning. Don't let her run off with you."

"I haven't forgotten how since yesterday," she snapped. "Heel!"

"You're right," Aaron said. "It's none of my business. But I want you to know that you don't have to worry about me. If you want to rob the cradle, I'd be the last one to criticize. Live and let live, I always say."

"You *say* a lot more than I'm interested in hearing."

"Why should age make a difference either way?" Aaron continued, oblivious. "Men have been coupling with younger women for centuries. Why shouldn't women enjoy younger lovers?''

"Halt!" Judy said, tugging at Fluffy's leash as she planted her feet on the sidewalk. "I don't know why I feel compelled to tell you this, but Gregory Simpson and I are not lovers. We're neighbors. And friends."

Aaron cocked an eyebrow at her. "Like you and I?"

"You and I are neighbors and acquaintances."

"How can you call a man who has shared an experience as intimate as training a dog with you a mere acquaintance?''

"Heel, Fluffy. It gets easier all the time. Now, as you can see, I'm doing very well with Fluffy, so there's no reason for you to waste your time hanging around with us."

"I was hoping I could try Fluffy on some of the doggie biscuits while you tossed that salad. Maybe teach her to sit."

Judy ignored him pointedly. Couldn't this clown take a hint? What did he want from her, anyway? And why did he have to be so devastatingly good-looking?

"It's been a long time since I had pizza," he said.

Again Judy ignored him, letting the silence expand between them until, hopefully, it penetrated his thick skin and he noticed that he was being ignored.

"Supreme is my favorite."

"Halt, Fluffy. Look J. Hollis—"

"Aaron. Just plain Aaron," he said irritably.

"I have a whole stack of coupons from pizza parlors in my kitchen. I'll be happy to give you the lot. Orlando is full of pizza places. You can take your pick."

"But I hate eating alone."

"Heel. Do you mind telling me why you've zeroed in on me?" Judy said. "There must be a gaggle of women who'd stand in line to go out with you."

Aaron snickered. "A gaggle?"

"A collective noun referring to a flock."

"Of geese."

"It doesn't matter to me who—or what—you take to eat pizza. If geese turn you on, I hope an endless supply of them go waddling through your life."

Score one for the lady, Aaron thought. "You manipulated that quite well," he said.

"I thought so."

After a beat of silence, Aaron threw back his head and guffawed. Judy stopped her walking just to look at him in awe. It was so unexpected, this burst of humor, this ability to laugh at himself. And his laughter was so deep, so spontaneous, so utterly masculine.

Watch yourself, she warned, realizing that she was warming to him, responding to the maleness of him on a very elemental level, wondering out of the blue what his cheek would feel like if she ran her fingers over it, whether the area he shaved would be rough or smooth. But he was not the type of man she wanted or needed. He was still on the treadmill she'd stepped off years ago, and she wasn't prepared to climb back on that treadmill for him or any other man.

She commanded the dog to heel and started walking. Aaron followed and caught up with her, and for a while they walked along in silence.

"Why don't you tell me what you're doing in Florida," she said finally.

"I was transferred."

"I meant the real reason."

"Do you always speak in riddles?" he said.

"No one leaves Wall Street without a valid reason. The salaries here aren't that competitive, and there's no place to progress to from here except back to New York."

"Would you believe I got tired of freezing my tush off all winter?"

"Maybe. But don't ask me to believe warm winters are enough to lure a man like you away from the excitement of daily contact with the New York Stock Exchange."

Aaron remembered the ugly scene with Melissa, the awkwardness of running into her when he least expected it, the realization that one of them had to leave and that fair play dictated it should be him. "I just needed a change of scenery."

"Very interesting," Judy said thoughtfully.

"That I needed a change of scenery?"

"That you find sticking your nose into my private life so easy, but you're very uncomfortable discussing yours."

"I just told you—"

"Obviously you aren't ready to talk about her yet."

"Halt," he said, and grasped her hand in his, yanking upward on the leash to stop the dog. Judy looked at him expectantly. "You enjoy baiting me, don't you?" he said.

"Forget I asked. It was none of my business. If I'd known it was such a sensitive subject I wouldn't have asked."

"I'm trying to make friends with you," he said, his voice taut. "Why don't you meet me halfway?"

Judy looked up at him, at the golden-blond hair draped elegantly over his forehead, at his patrician nose, at the stubborn set of his jaw as he waited for the answer he had demanded. "It might be best," she said, "if we just remained acquaintances."

"Why?" he asked, and she could see the distress in his eyes. Men accustomed to knowing all the answers didn't like not knowing them.

"Because I don't like men who come barging into my life trying to run it," she said. *And because right now I'm wondering what it would feel like to have you kiss me.*

"I don't—"

"Yes, you do. But I don't think you do it on purpose. You do it because . . . well, because full speed ahead is the only way you know how to do anything."

Aaron's arms were folded across his waist. His voice was cynical. "Is this a hobby with you, or will I get a bill for this personality analysis?"

"I wouldn't charge for anything so obvious." She tugged at the leash. "Heel, Fluffy."

Aaron walked along beside her in exasperated silence. He did not know how to deal with her—her cheekiness, her haughtiness, her incisive perception that left him feeling exposed and off-center. He was supposed to be seducing her away from Gregory, but he was striking out every time he stepped up to the plate. His jaw set with marblelike hardness, and his mouth straightened into a grim line. The game wasn't over yet; there were innings left to play.

"Why me?" he said.

She cast him a sideways glance. "Why you what?"

"Why did you choose me as the target for that big chip on your shoulder? Every time I get within throwing distance you fling it at me."

"I'm not sure I know which chip you mean—would you describe it for me?" she said.

"It's big and it's heavy and it hurts when it hits," he replied.

She had the most phenomenal smile. She was not beautiful, but when she smiled her face was striking, interesting. Lush, full lips formed an enchanting frame for the porcelain perfection of large, even teeth. Aaron was intrigued by her mouth, by the contrast between the lovely sensitivity of her smile and the waspish comments she was so capable of hurling at him through those same lips.

Aaron could think of better uses for those full lips than having them form acerbic barbs aimed at his ego. But he refused to be charmed out of his pique by a smile. He wasn't going to let the sexiest mouth south of the Appalachian mountains disrupt his concentration in the middle of a game—a most intriguing game, and one he intended to win. "What is it, Judy?" he asked. "Has some man hurt you, or has life in general kicked you around?"

He saw the question hit home, striking her like a physical blow and wilting the smile, and felt a stab of remorse at having been so ruthless. She stopped abruptly, forgetting even to command the dog to halt. "You didn't discuss your private life," she said. "I don't care to discuss mine."

After they had glared at each other a few seconds, Aaron lifted her chin with his forefinger. "Would you consider a cease-fire, Miss Harte?"

Treadmill Clone or not, J. Hollis Aaron was a stunningly handsome man, and Judy reacted to his looks and the warm perusal of his sapphire-blue eyes the way any healthy, red-blooded woman would. A stab of sexual awareness zinged through her, shocking her senses with its unexpectedness. She was very conscious of the pressure of his finger where it touched her, of the masculine roughness of his skin against the velvety smoothness of her own. And she saw in the vast blue depths of his eyes a glint of sexual yearning equal to her own.

Was he as surprised by it as she? Judy wondered. He'd been flirting with her ever since he'd met her, but she'd gotten the impression that it was because he was lonely and she was convenient. What was happening between them now was intensely personal. Was he feeling it, too?

"We're neighbors," she said. "We'll be running into each other from time to time. I suppose a bilateral cessation of hostilities would make sense."

The sexual glint was still in his eyes, but there was a hint of mischief in his smile. "How do we seal this pact?"

"Cutting our fingers and letting our blood flow together seems a bit dramatic."

"An old-fashioned handshake?"

"I don't need it in writing if you don't." And so they shook hands, with Aaron's large, strong hand closing firmly around hers. A firm handshake would be a reflex with him, Judy thought, a tool of his trade connoting confidence and sincerity. "Trust me," it would tell clients. "Give me your money, and I'll take care of it. I know how."

Oh yes, Judy thought, glowing in the light of his charming smile. She would trust J. Hollis Aaron with her money if she had any to invest. Her heart was a different matter. She only hoped that he settled for friendship, because the way she was feeling at the moment she might offer her heart to him on a platter if he asked for it.

They finished circling the courtyard and returned to Judy's condo. Aaron opened the doggie biscuits and, taking a chair at the table in the breakfast nook that adjoined the kitchen, fed a couple of them to Fluffy while Judy washed her hands and took salad fixings from the refrigerator.

"I'm going to teach her to sit," Aaron said. "Watch so you can do this several times a day. She'll love it."

Judy left the vegetables to drain while she turned to watch. "Sit!" Aaron said, and pushed Fluffy's rump to the ground. He waited a few seconds and fed the dog a treat. Excited, Fluffy jumped up. "Sit!" Aaron repeated, pushing on her rump again. Then, to Judy, he said, "Just keep repeating the command and enforcing it, and eventually she'll catch on that when you tell her to sit you mean for her to stay put.'' He praised the dog and gave her another biscuit.

He was actually fond of the dog, Judy realized. She had assumed—unfairly, it seemed—that his interest in training dogs was centered around his need to be in control. ''You enjoy working with her, don't you?'' she said.

''Yes,'' he said. ''My father and I always kept a couple of dogs on the estate.''

''The estate?''

He laughed. ''Sounds impressive, doesn't it? My mother called it that to tease my father. I guess times were pretty lean for them when he was in medical school.''

So his father was a doctor. Judy wasn't surprised.

''It's really a rambling house and several acres in Connecticut,'' Aaron continued. ''We had a stable and a couple of horses and a couple of dogs. I had a goat once, too. Houdini,'' he said, grinning self-consciously because she smiled at the name. ''We thought the name was very cute when we bought him, but I had to give him away when we found out it was very apropos and we couldn't keep him penned. He kept getting in my mother's flower beds. I slept in the barn two nights in a row to protest having to give him up.''

''How old were you then?''

''Eleven,'' he said.

''And you already liked having your own way,'' she said. Were Treadmill Clones born or developed?

''I disliked losing a treasured pet,'' he said defensively. ''Houdini was like a friend, a brother almost. I was crushed. I thought my mother was being totally unreasonable—what were a few flowers compared to a goat like

Houdini?'' With a sheepish chuckle he added, ''A few *award-winning* hybrid flowers.''

''Are you still harboring a grudge?''

Aaron frowned. ''Not over Houdini.'' His voice told her it was a closed subject—and a sensitive one.

So he and his mother didn't get along, Judy thought. Turning back to the vegetables in the sink, she said, ''Why didn't you become a doctor like your father?''

''The prospect of cutting people open and fooling around with muscle and bone always seemed a little ludicrous to me. I didn't have the calling or the stomach for it. I ruled out veterinary medicine for the same reason.''

''So you went to Harvard and earned an M.B.A.''

''I went to *Yale* for an M.B.A.,'' he said irritably.

Turning to face him and discovering a brooding scowl contorting his face, Judy was struck by the absurdity of it and giggled. ''I'm sorry. I didn't mean to insult you.''

His scowl didn't soften, which only amused her more. ''Honestly, J. Hollis, I didn't know you went to Yale,'' she said. ''Yalies and Harvard men all look alike to me.''

''I don't know what you find so amusing,'' he said as he watched her succumb to full-scale laughter.

''*That's* what's so amusing.''

Aaron felt the exasperation rising in him, filling him, and was perplexed by it. He didn't know how to deal with her irreverent ridicule, her blatant lack of respect for the things he considered important. He continued glowering at her but found himself thinking, in spite of his outrage, that she was beautiful when laughter brightened her eyes.

Trying to swallow her laughter, Judy walked over to him and put her hand on his shoulder. ''I'm sorry,'' she said. ''It just struck me as funny.'' He stood up, and was suddenly very near her, closer to her than he'd ever been.

"Because I wasn't trying to tease you and I struck such a responsive—"

His face, still contorted by a menacing scowl, was just inches from hers. His eyes drew hers, held them. Breathing became a conscious chore for her. The scent of his after-shave filled her nostrils and reverberated through her senses. She swallowed and finished lamely, "—chord."

His hands came up to close around the tops of her arms, and for a moment he just looked down at her, the scowl metamorphosing into something different, not menacing but equally volatile.

She knew instinctively the instant he decided to kiss her, and she knew in the same instant that she wanted his arms around her, his lips on hers. They moved together, each conceding half the distance between them as though they'd agreed to meet in neutral territory. His arms slid around her shoulders, and she let hers glide around his waist. His body was warm and hard as she melded into his embrace and held her breath in anticipation of his lips touching hers.

A sense of urgency overwhelmed them, catching them by surprise. Aaron had not expected her to feel so good in his arms. He usually dated tall women, and the full curves of her body aligned with his in a way that was unique and quite pleasant.

To Judy, the world was momentarily reduced to dimensions large enough to encompass only Aaron's warmth and the sensations his touch evoked in her. The intensity of the feelings spreading through her perplexed her, but she was too engrossed in the kiss to question it.

The doorbell was a rude intrusion on their privacy. Aaron drew away from Judy and looked down at her with a puzzled expression on his face. Judy took a deep breath, swallowed and said, "That must be Gregory with the pizza."

"Ah, yes, it must be Gregory—with the pizza." He brushed his lips over hers briefly before taking his arms from around her.

"Hope you're as hungry as I am," Gregory said, stepping through the door the moment Judy opened it. "This pizza smells delicious. It was driving me crazy in the—" He stopped in midsentence when he stepped into the kitchen and spied Aaron. "Oh, hi," he said with barely concealed hostility. A beat too late he tried to cover his sullen rudeness by asking, "How did the training session go?"

"Very nicely," Aaron said, reaching down to pat Fluffy. "She's doing fine."

"I was just trying to talk J. Hollis into staying for pizza," Judy said.

Aaron's jaw almost dropped in shock, and he raised his eyebrow skeptically, as if to ask, *Is* that *what you were doing?*

The petulance that had hardened the lines of Gregory's mouth earlier returned. "Sure," he said, though not graciously. "If you'd like to stay. There's plenty, and it's supreme without the anchovies, the way you suggested."

"As I was just telling Judy," Aaron said, "I couldn't possibly stay tonight." He smiled broadly. "I'll take a rain check, though. Soon."

It was Judy's turn to be flabbergasted. How dare he bow out so gallantly after practically trying to bulldoze an invitation earlier!

An awkward three-way silence ensued, but Aaron ended it astutely. "I'm sure you two want to eat while your pizza's hot," he said, turning to leave.

Judy followed him to the door. "You could have stayed," she said, unsure herself whether it was a statement, a complaint or an accusation. Still reeling from the effect of the kiss they had shared, she perceived his leaving as an abandonment, as though he were walking off in the middle of an argument.

"Two's company, three's..." He let the sentence trail off as his eyes roamed over her face in a perusal that was frankly sexual.

"I told you it's not like that with Gregory and me."

"Maybe you're trying to convince the wrong person."

The silence that followed was strained. Finally Judy said, "Thank you for the doggie biscuits."

Aaron smiled. "Maybe I'll run into you tomorrow while you're working with Fluffy."

Judy smiled back. "Maybe so."

After placing a brief, utterly platonic kiss on her cheek, Aaron left.

Confusion was the only emotion Judy could positively identify as she watched him walk away.

Chapter Four

Witch's toenails! Judy thought, catching sight of J. Hollis walking toward her on the sidewalk. She'd thought she'd managed to avoid him by walking Fluffy right after school, but there he was, dashingly good-looking in a tailored suit and smiling a smile that did crazy things to her pulse rate despite her resolve to maintain an air of cool detachment toward him.

Two minutes either way and she would have missed him—two lousy, disgusting minutes! *Ah, well,* she thought, feeling an involuntary smile forming on her lips, *might as well accept the inevitable with aplomb.*

"Where's your fuzzy sidekick?" he asked.

"I walked her earlier," Judy answered. "She did very well. I tried putting a little more slack on the leash, and she still stayed right with me."

His eyes roved over her face with explicit appreciation. "I was hoping..." Aaron left the sentence dangling, unsure exactly what he'd been hoping but aware of disappointment welling inside him because he'd planned on dropping by her condo, walking the dog and cajoling Judy into going to dinner with him. He told himself it was so he could assure Virginia Simpson that he was earnestly trying to steer Judy away from Gregory, but he wasn't naive enough to believe a whopper of a lie like that, regardless of the source. Judy Harte piqued his interest, haunted his thoughts in unguarded moments. And that had nothing to do with Virginia Simpson.

"You were hoping?" Judy prompted.

Aaron snapped out of the trance he had wandered into. "Hoping I could entice you to have dinner with me tonight."

Judy had to get away from him. She could feel her resistance to his charm melting in the warmth radiating from his smile. "I was just leaving," she said.

"Off for a night of fun and frolic?" he asked, eyeing her sweat suit skeptically.

"Off to the gym, actually," she said.

"You work out?"

Judy grinned at the incredulity in his voice. So he didn't think she worked out, huh? Mischievously she stood on tiptoe and whispered in his ear, "Under these baggy sweats resides a body hard as tempered steel."

Nothing she could have said—not the standard sweet nothings, not some blatant proposition—would have surprised him more or affected him as instantly or intensely. His mind filled with memories of how she had felt when he'd held her in his arms, not like tempered steel at all, but warm, full and womanly-pliant. His mouth suddenly was dry as cotton, and he was fighting valiantly *not* to think about what was going on in certain other parts of his anatomy. *This* hadn't been part of his deal with Mrs. Simpson.

"Where do you go?" he asked.

"Work and Play."

"Do you like it? Is it a good gym?"

"It's . . . yes, I enjoy it. I just do the machines, then go to the water aerobics."

"Is it coed?"

Damn, Judy thought, knowing where the question was heading. "Yes."

"I've been planning on finding a gym. Why don't I go with you. They give visitors' tours, don't they?"

"Yes, but—"

"What time is your water class?"

"Seven," she said, knowing she was sunk when he glanced at his watch.

"It won't take me ten minutes to get into my workout clothes. Come on to my place and wait."

Why was she going? she wondered as his hand cupped her elbow and hurried her along. What more appropriate place to go with a Treadmill Clone than a gym? she thought, smiling wryly.

His living room was traditionally furnished and unexpectedly cozy. Following his admonition to make herself at home, she explored the room to satisfy some perverse curiosity about him. The collection of books stored in the open bookcase was eclectic: thrillers, reference books on financial theory, a dictionary, a collection of poetry. Judy picked up the volume of poetry, which was utterly out of place with the other titles, and it fell open to the title page, where an inscription was written in a bold, feminine hand: "To inspire you. Love, Melissa." It was dated Christmas of the previous year.

Embarrassed by a sudden feeling of voyeurism, she snapped the book shut and replaced it on the shelf. Was Melissa the reason he'd left New York? *It's none of your business,* she reminded herself, trying not to wonder who Melissa was, trying to convince herself that she didn't *care* who Melissa was or about any of the women J. Hollis Aaron had been involved with as long as her own name didn't wind up on the list.

A painting over the mantel drew her attention: two men in corduroy pants and flannel shirts walking through a field of tall grass. A stand of trees clothed in autumn-hued leaves formed a backdrop for the portrait, and two dogs with long golden coats nipped at the men's booted feet. The painting was not detailed enough to show specific facial features, but the men resembled J. Hollis in a general coloring and build, one a younger version of him, the other an older one. The mood of the portrait was one of serenity, repleteness.

"It was done from a photograph," Aaron said, catching her in the act of appreciation.

"You and your father?" Judy guessed.

"Yes."

"On the estate?"

He laughed at her use of the word. "Yes."

Judy was still studying the portrait. "You look content."

"We were. We'd been out walking for hours that day. Usually about the time we got out in the fields my dad's beeper would go off and he'd be off on some emergency consultation."

"The busy life of a country doctor?"

Aaron laughed. "Hardly. He's an orthopedic surgeon. Every time there's a weird bone break in New England ski country Aaron is the specialist called in."

"It must have been difficult for you, having him so preoccupied with his work."

"I was used to it," Aaron said. "It was just the way things were." Standing behind Judy, he put his hands on her shoulders. "My father was an important man, and people needed him. He cared about them but he loved us. We knew the difference." Judy felt the seductive warmth of his body against her back and fought the temptation to relax against his strength.

"Who took the photograph?"

"My mom. She happened to see us when she was working in the garden, and took it with a telephoto lens. I guess that's why we're so relaxed."

Was it because he didn't see the camera, or because he didn't see his mother watching? she wondered. But his mother was a closed subject. "The estate looks lovely," she said, letting her shoulder blades brush his chest.

A note of nostalgia was audible in his voice. "Autumn was always the prettiest time of year there."

"Speaking of time..." she said, tilting her head back so it grazed his shoulder.

"Ah, yes. Time to hone the body of steel."

"Why do I detect a hint of irony when you say that?"

His laughter was musical. "Because I've never known steel to be huggable."

"And I'm huggable?"

"Eminently," he said, crossing his arms over her chest above her breasts.

With a soft sigh, Judy relaxed, finally letting her body meld into the warmth and strength of his. He pressed a fleeting, teasing kiss on her temple. "We could work out here," he whispered, his voice smooth and seductive in her ear.

It was a tempting prospect. Cloistered in his arms, Judy felt curiously safe and warm. She had only to turn in that magic circle of strength and slip her arms around his waist and let him teach her lessons of which she was sure he was a skilled master, and at which she was a fledgling novice. Instead she pulled away from him, forcing his arms apart as she broke loose of the inviting circle they made.

"Your bathtub's not deep enough for water aerobics," she said lightly, scurrying ahead of him toward the door. When she decided to go to bed with a man, it would be because he'd invited her personally—because he wanted to share something special with Judy Harte—not because he'd cast out a haphazard suggestion hoping he would get lucky with a woman who happened to be convenient when he got the urge. For all she knew, he might be looking for some outlet for his frustration over missing Melissa, whoever the hell Melissa was.

Aaron followed her, relieved that she didn't seem offended by his sudden proposition. Actually, most of him was glad she had treated the suggestion as a joke and tactfully refused him. Certain parts of him still burned with the stimulation that had prompted the outrageous suggestion in the first place, but the thinking part of him realized that the situation surrounding Judy Harte was growing more complicated with his attraction to her, and a sexual liaison would only complicate it further. When he'd taken on this dastardly assignment of Virginia Simpson's, he'd planned on dealing with a conniving little gold digger; instead he'd found Judy—bouncy, guileless, irreverent, caustic-tongued but soft as dandelion fluff under the illusory shell of armor she wore.

When he'd agreed to romance her, he hadn't planned on liking her. He was trapped between the proverbial rock and a hard place, torn between conscience and duty, confused because the two seemed to overlap until he couldn't distinguish one from the other.

Conscience over what, duty to whom? He wasn't sure anymore. Only one fact emerged in this mishmash of shoulds, ought-tos and wants: he had to get out from under his commitment to Virginia Simpson. Now that he'd gotten to know Judy, the idea of her trying to seduce Gregory Simpson seemed as ridiculous as it was ludicrous, and he planned to tell Virginia Simpson that at the earliest opportunity.

"Nice car," Judy said as they settled into the front seat of his Volvo, thinking, *Of course he has a nice car, a prestigious car with a solid reputation for performance. A car is an extension of the Treadmill Clone's identity.*

"I use it a lot more now than in New York. I don't know which is the bigger hassle—parking in New York or traffic in Orlando."

Judy laughed. "It won't take you long to figure it out."

The spa was only a few minutes away. Judy signed in and introduced Aaron to Laurie, who was manning the desk. Laurie greeted Aaron enthusiastically, with the energy that was characteristic of the entire Work and Play staff, and warmed to him even more when she learned he was a prospective member.

"I hate to abandon you," Judy said to Aaron, "but I've just got time to get out of these sweats before my class. It's a small spa. You should be able to find me when you're ready to leave."

Before Aaron could reply, Laurie piped in, "Don't worry. We'll take good care of him. We're not going to let him get lost." She slid a card across the countertop as Aaron watched Judy disappear behind a swinging door that led to the main hall. "Just fill this out for me, Aaron, and I'll give you the grand tour."

Laurie was wearing top-of-the-line workout chic, matching iridescent blue tights and leotards that hugged her lean body like a second skin. Her auburn hair was short and slightly spiked above the sweatband she wore on her forehead, and when she smiled two cavernous dimples appeared in her cheeks. There was a glint in her eye, too, Aaron noted, a slightly predatory gleam of availability that sparkled when she looked up after reading the card he'd filled out and instructed him to follow her for a tour of the facilities.

She was exactly his type physically. He thought idly that he should be flirting with her, but he felt only a detached appreciation for her physical perfection as he followed her into the weight room and listened to her bubbling commentary on the marvels of high-tech weight machinery.

The workout studio was next on the tour, a brightly lit room with mirrored walls, an elevated platform for the instructor and a sophisticated stereo system that was belching rock music. A coed class was doing sit-ups in time to the beat of the music under the staccato commands and encouragement of the instructor.

"We have fourteen classes daily," Laurie told Aaron, leaning close to him to speak directly in his ear so she would be heard over the music. "You'll get a schedule."

It was a relief to step back into the hall, where the glass walls muted the music to a tolerable noise level. "Here's the men's locker room, if you'd like to go in and look around," Laurie said. She chuckled. "They don't let me in this one."

Metal lockers. Wooden benches with scrapes in the paint. A few socks balled up in obscure corners. A pervading odor of sweat and soap. Aaron didn't linger. No need to keep Laurie waiting while he absorbed the sights, sounds and smells of a locker room.

The pool area enclosed a pool and a hot tub. Laurie was explaining the controls for the hot tub when Aaron spied

Judy in a cluster of women standing at the pool's edge. Her back was to him, but he recognized the proliferation of ash-brown curls dancing over her bare shoulders.

He had not thought of her as statuesque, but he revised his thinking as his eyes roved over the full length of her body. She was short, true, with full hips and breasts, but the swimsuit clung to a figure that was hourglass perfect. She might not be molded from tempered steel, but her muscles were well toned, and despite her feminine roundness she was not carrying any excess weight.

A brunette wearing a Work and Play T-shirt over her swimsuit entered the area, walked briskly to the edge of the pool and blew the whistle that dangled from a plastic braid rope around her neck. "Time to make the plunge, ladies!" she announced.

The cluster of women with whom Judy had been talking dispersed and, one by one, entered the water via the corner steps or a single bold leap into the shallow end. Judy caught sight of Aaron, smiled and waved as she jumped into the water. He smiled and waved back, unwittingly staring at her as she tilted her head from side to side at the instructor's command. The sound of a throat being cleared with purpose drew his attention back to Laurie. "Sorry," he said. "I was just curious about the water class."

"It's coed, if you're interested in participating."

His soft chortle validated her skepticism. "The steam room and sauna are over here," she said. "Have you ever used either?"

"Both. I belonged to a club in New York."

"Then I don't have to go through the precautions and instructions, which are posted on the door, anyway. You might want to skim over them before using either of the rooms."

"I will."

She led him back to the hall. "That's the tour. Are you interested in learning about our membership plans?"

"Might as well take care of business," he said, and followed her to the small office where he filled out the membership forms and wrote out the necessary check. From there he went to the locker room and on to the weight room. It had been a month since he'd worked out, so he started slowly and didn't push himself as hard as usual. Still, he worked until his body was shimmering with the sweat of physical exertion and his hair was coiled into damp ringlets. The exertion was exhilarating, the perspiration cleansing to his mind as well as his body. He became immersed in the challenge of lifting and holding, concentrating on the mastery of human strength over gravity and mindless mass, of strength over weakness.

The air was chilly as Judy stepped from the heated pool when her class was over. Shivering, she walked to the hot tub and sank gratefully into its warm, bubbling depths. For a few moments she tilted her head back and closed her eyes, letting the churning water knead the muscles she'd taxed during her workout. When she opened them, she gazed idly through the window in front of the tub, which was directly across from the open door to the free weight room where Aaron was working with weights. Ordinarily she wasn't impressed by raw brawn, but she seemed unable to look away from the intriguing sight of J. Hollis Aaron working with barbells. The sleekness of muscles that glimmered with the sheen of hard labor mesmerized her, and the concentration that she recognized as a symptom of his treadmill personality fascinated her, demanding a grudging respect.

Knowing he was too involved in what he was doing to notice her, she continued watching him, marveling at the enigma that a man who was so Wall Street could also turn out to be so physical. And even more enigmatic was the fact that the two types of men she found least appealing— the Treadmill Clones and the lean, brawny ones—when combined into one man became strangely irresistible.

She closed her eyes again, but the image of Aaron's lean, hard body lingered in her mind. Perhaps his allure was linked to the fact that he had admitted he found her huggable, and she had felt the undeniable evidence that he found her desirable as well when she'd let her body meld against his in an embrace.

As he left the weight room, Aaron spotted her through the window. She was perfectly relaxed, and her head was tilted back at an angle that made him want to nibble on her neck. He entered the pool area, peeled off his muscle shirt and stepped under the shower that was a prerequisite for entering either the pool or the hot tub. At the edge of the hot tub, he touched the top of Judy's head to get her attention.

Opening her eyes, she smiled up at him lazily. "Oh. It's you. Hi."

You were expecting the ghost of Rudolph Valentino? he thought ruefully before replying, "Hi, yourself. How about a few laps in the pool?"

"I've already done my laps. Now I'm luxuriating." Her sigh was decidedly feline.

"Stay put, then, and I'll luxuriate with you as soon as I've done mine."

Stay put, Judy mimicked in her mind. Mr. Treadmill Clone certainly took a lot for granted giving her orders!

He joined her a few minutes later, melting into the soothing massage of the swirling water as though he might die of pleasure. "It feels good to work out again." Closing his eyes, he tilted his head back and exhaled heavily. "I think."

The irritation Judy had been harboring dissolved in the face of his very human display of fatigue. "Maybe you'd better wait until tomorrow to decide," she said wryly.

Aaron groaned. "Don't remind me."

"I won't have to. Your muscles will do that."

"Sadist," he said.

"Sorry. I'm not into any of the kinky stuff."

His eyes opened and lethargically studied her face, then moved down to her neck and the cleavage revealed by the snug top of her swimsuit before moving back up.

The water in the hot tub suddenly seemed hotter, the steam thicker. Considering that he hadn't said word, Judy thought wryly, he certainly was a master communicator.

"How do you feel about healthy heterosexual encounters between consenting adults?" he asked. His voice sounded as though it had passed through a velvet-lined windpipe.

"Is that a generic question, or did you have a specific pair of consenting adults in mind?"

He traced her profile with his forefinger, starting in the center of her forehead and following the bridge of her nose, pausing briefly on her lips before continuing over her chin to her neck. He became very aware of the rise and fall of her breasts as the pace of her breathing altered. "The question was very specific, Miss Harte."

"Consenting is the operative word," she said.

"And what is your position on consent?"

His double entendre skittered across her taut nerve endings, and she threw back her head and laughed. "After consent, position is negotiable."

Looking at her beautiful mouth, the full, sensuous lips and straight, perfect teeth, Aaron wasn't sure whether he

would like most to strangle her for laughing in the middle
of a seduction or kiss her into submission. Kissing, he decided, would be the procedure of choice. He forced a smile
while silently cursing the fact that they weren't alone. "I
asked a specific question and got a generic answer," he
complained.

"I find generic quite comfortable, thank you," Judy
said. She needed space, perspective. He was getting to her,
reaching her with his velvet voice and his butterfly-soft
touch. The sensation of his finger dancing over her skin
and hovering over her lips was still strong in her memory,
and her thinking was getting fuzzy.

"I've been in this water so long that I'm going to shrivel
up. I'm going to get dressed." She stood, welcoming the
shock of cool air against her warm, moist skin. A little chill
could be a good thing for one's perspective.

An involuntary groan hissed through Aaron's lips as her
hips, closely hugged by her suit, passed within inches of his
face as she stepped out of the tub. "I'll meet you at the
desk," he said, offering a silent prayer of thanks that
women inevitably took longer to dress than men. It was
going to be a while before he was going to be able to walk
from the hot tub to the dressing room without embarrassing himself.

"Interesting reading?"

Aaron looked up from the schedule of classes and
smiled. He slid his arm across Judy's shoulders as they left
the building. "Quite interesting. Did you know that the
very class I'd like to take—the challenge workout—happens to be offered at the exact time of your water aerobics?" He leaned close to her and whispered in her ear,
"We could be riding to the spa together regularly."

The intimacy he took for granted, the brassy assumption in his attitude irritated her. Full speed ahead. The only speed at which a Treadmill Clone traveled. J. Hollis undoubtedly went after investment opportunities with the same tunnel-visioned, goal-oriented directness with which he was trying to get her into his bed.

Judy frowned while he walked around his car after opening the passenger door for her. She didn't doubt that he found her attractive, but she harbored no illusions that she was special to him. He was lonely and she was convenient. It was sometimes difficult for her to remember that when she was under the spell of the sensual smolder in his blue eyes and his practiced techniques of seduction. The intimate whispers, the cozy little caresses and the deliberate smiles were weakening the seams of her resistance.

I do find you attractive, she admitted silently, grudgingly, as he settled into the driver's seat. *But please let us be just friends.* It would be better to be friends than lovers with a man with whom she had nothing and no one in common, wouldn't it?

Lovers? When had she begun thinking of him as a potential lover? He must have found a weak seam and penetrated her resistance without her realizing it. The idea of being seduced by J. Hollis Aaron was not as preposterous as it should have been. When she asked herself, "Why him, of all people?" the first answer she heard was, "If you're going to take the plunge, why not with him? He's rather magnificent."

It was only after reason overcame chemistry that she heard the small voice warning her that he'd break her heart.

"Where shall we go for dinner?" he asked, lowering his hand over hers as it lay in her lap. His clasp was strong on her hands as his fingers wrapped around hers, his knuckles hot as they branded the top of her thigh through the fleece of her sweatpants.

The sudden intimacy of his touch stunned her, and she felt transparent, as though he could look inside her head and see what she was thinking. *He knows,* she thought. *Damn him, he knows I was sitting here weighing the pros and cons of becoming his lover.* And then it was devastatingly clear to her that he thought he already had the battle won. *Just a matter of time,* he was telling himself.

"I can't go out to eat dressed like this," she said brusquely, unconsciously squaring her shoulders against the back of the seat.

"Like what?"

"Come on, Mr. Pin-striped Suit. I'm dressed for the *gym,* not a dining room."

What was it with this woman? Aaron thought, stinging from the sharpness of her unexpected attack. Every time he got close to her, she bared her claws—or that equally sharp tongue of hers. "I wasn't planning on the dining room at the Hyatt," he said. "There are casual restaurants, you know. I'm not exactly wearing a tie."

"*You* are wearing a color-coordinated ensemble designed for well-dressed rising executives who want to keep their images intact while keeping their bodies in shape. And I—"

Without consciously deciding to do so, Aaron slammed on the brakes and made a sharp turn into the deserted parking lot of an office park. The scowl on his face as he turned to her was thunderous. Judy stared back at him with the wide eyes of a startled animal, dry-throated, frozen in place as she waited for the thunderbolt of unadulterated anger to come crashing down around her.

"*You,*" he said, nearly shouting, "are purposely picking a fight, for heaven only knows why, and I refuse to fight with you. You've got on a perfectly nice jogging suit, your hair is drying out all fluffy, and you smell..."

Neither of them could have pinpointed the moment his arms went around her, when one hand pressed into the center of her back pulling her close to him and the other thrust through her damp hair to tilt her head back, the instant his tirade fizzled into a kiss. They were just there suddenly, touching each other, kissing, tasting, hungrily feasting on sensations. His victory was utterly complete. When he lifted his lips from hers and clasped her against the breadth of his chest and burrowed his face in her hair, she was limp and devoid of resistance, hostility and wariness. Their breathing, their very heartbeats seemed peculiarly synchronized in the dark silence of the car.

"What *is* that you're wearing?" he asked, his chest still heaving against her cheek with each indrawn breath.

Her voice was soft, with a faraway quality. "It's called Allure. I... they were giving away samples at the perfume counter the last time I was at the mall. I...I think I'll save up and buy a bottle. It seems... to work."

His laughter—deep, resonant, unrestrained—wafted melodically through the car. "I'll buy you a bottle for Christmas." They both heard his mind silently finish the statement: *If you'll wear it with me.*

"Now where are we going for dinner?" he asked after the brief silence in the car threatened to become unpleasant. "If you don't give me a suggestion, I'm stopping at the first hole-in-the-wall I see."

Her outrage at his manipulation had mysteriously dissolved with his laughter. She knew she was trapped into having dinner with him but didn't begrudge him the victory. She tried to imagine him in a hole-in-the-wall and couldn't. It would be just too cruel to put a man like J. Hollis Aaron in a dingy dive somewhere. Accepting that, and worrying that he might be crueler than she and stop somewhere she'd feel terribly underdressed and conspicuous, she asked, "American with a salad bar or Chinese?"

"I had salad for lunch."

She gave him directions as he drove. A modest sign was the only thing that heralded the existence of Ming's restaurant in the forlorn little strip of shops that adjoined a Publix supermarket. When he had turned off the engine, Aaron gave her a look that suggested he wondered if she might have purposely brought him to a hole-in-the-wall through some perverse need to goad him.

"The food's excellent," she quickly assured him. "Honest."

They ordered à la carte and shared bits and bites of everything with Ming's fried rice. They talked about everything and nothing without trespassing on each other's private lives or invading each other's private thoughts, yet Judy remained aware of some intangible force working between them, drawing them together, a milder genus of the same force that had sparked between them earlier in the car when fury had flared into passion.

At the end of their meal the waitress, a pretty Chinese woman who nodded a lot to compensate for the English she understood very little of, served the check and pair of complimentary fortune cookies on a tiny lacquer tray. Judy picked one up, broke it open and read the fortune with grave concentration.

Aaron reached across the table to cover her hand with his. "Does it say a tall fair man thinks you're stunning?"

She gifted him with a smile, a rare, open smile that gladdened his heart. "It says..." She paused for dramatic effect, then pretended to read, "'Beware of Connecticut Yankees who could break your heart.'"

"It doesn't," he said, laughing.

"It does," she insisted, mischief dancing in her eyes. "What does yours say?"

Snapping the cookie into two perfect halves, he pulled out the tiny slip of paper, read it and nonchalantly cast it aside. "J. Hollis!" she prompted, exasperated, and when he lifted his eyebrows as though he had no idea what she was asking, she added, "What did it say?"

His grip on her hand tightened perceptibly, and a proprietary gleam glistened in his blue eyes. Uncomfortable, Judy wanted to look away but couldn't.

"It said," he told her, " 'When a wise man finds something good, he does not let it go.' " And then, as though it had just occurred to him and he was surprised by what he was saying, he said, "You're good, aren't you, Judy."

With sudden, blinding realization, he understood that. She was good and he, J. Hollis Aaron, was not good. He was cruel; he'd let himself become a pawn in a heartless game. He'd assumed the worst about Judy before he'd even met her and, without giving her the respect of one human being for another, had plotted to deceive and manipulate her.

Good? Judy wasn't quite sure what he meant. Was it a compliment? An endearment? Sexual innuendo beyond her realm of sophistication? She didn't know whether to ignore him, say "Thank you" or slap his face. Swallowing nervously, she started to move her hand from under his, only to have his fingers clamp around hers.

"Confucius said I should hold on to you," he said gravely. "And I'm not going to break your heart." He'd broken enough hearts for one man in a single lifetime. Judy Harte was not going to be added to the list of casualties; no one ever would again.

Judy held her breath as their eyes met, hers questioning, his staidly serious. Gradually a slow grin spread over his face, chasing away the ominous solemnity that had hovered over the moment. Relaxing, allowing her shoulders to glide back against the back of the banquette, she grinned at him. He was flirting, that's all. *Wasn't he?*

Aaron's eyes were still stubbornly fixed on her face as though he were memorizing it. He shifted restlessly, frowned and said, "It's time to leave." His hand squeezed hers tightly, almost punishingly before releasing it. A shiver of premonition crawled over his spine, an ill-defined, illogical fear that he might never touch her again. With it came the repulsive conviction that he didn't deserve to touch her. With his jaw clenched resolutely, he presented the bill and a credit card to the cashier, waited to write in the amount of the tip and then walked with Judy to the car.

He was going to call Mrs. Simpson the next day and demand to be set free of this dastardly commitment. When he courted Judy Harte, he wanted to do so without ulterior motives.

It was as though the awkwardness, the hostility that had sparked between them earlier had remained trapped in the car, coiled up there like a snake, hiding in a dark corner to spring between them again, Judy thought on the silent drive home. His sullen silence rebuked her. Was this the same man who had kissed her so passionately barely an hour ago and made such a game of holding her hand?

A game? Was that the truth of it? On close analysis, the interaction between them appeared to be a series of tumultuous challenges and counterchallenges. And this withdrawal wasn't unprecedented. He'd reacted much the same way yesterday, the first time he'd kissed her. Kiss and retreat. An ugly suspicion settled heavily in her chest, the suspicion that he was playing games with her, masculine Treadmill Clone power games.

"Why did you leave last night?" Her voice sounded tiny and weak even to her own ears, and she wondered what masochistic urge had led her to ask the question.

Chapter Five

Damn, but she had hellacious timing! The last thing Aaron needed when he was wallowing in guilt over deceiving her was to be reminded of his deception. A muscle in his cheek twitched as he clenched his already taut jaw tighter, and a frown tugged at his mouth as he suppressed a sigh of exasperation. Finally, while they were waiting at a red light, he looked at her. "You already had company."

"But I asked you to stay after..." *After you kissed me.* Having verbally painted herself into a corner, she exhaled a defeated sigh and tried again. "You could have stayed."

"You'd made it very clear that you didn't want a third wheel. Two's company and three's—"

"You said that yesterday, just before I explained to you that Gregory and I are not that kind of 'company.' And what exactly did you mean when you said that I was trying to convince the wrong person of that?"

"I meant that it's Gregory you should be convincing. The way he looks at you would make Antony's overtures to Cleopatra pale."

"It's just a crush. It happens with my students all the time."

"He's not a sixth-grader," Aaron said, accelerating the car a bit too zealously as the light turned green.

"He might as well be. He's nineteen."

"He's a foot taller than you!"

"He's also very nice looking and drives a fancier car than I do, but he's still just a kid."

"He's in love with you!"

"For Pete's sake, J. Hollis, I've been helping him with his homework. He's dazzled by my brilliance."

They had reached the condo complex. Thank God, Aaron muttered as he turned into the parking lot. "If you're so damned brilliant, would you *please* try to remember to call me Aaron? And are you really naive enough to think Gregory isn't old enough...that he hasn't noticed your—" he sniffed, exasperated "—face?"

The absurdity of his gallantry amused her. By the time he had walked around the car to open the door for her, what began as a gentle giggle had evolved into rollicking laughter. Feeling slightly drunk with the unexpected display of his jealousy, she put her hands on his shoulders to steady herself after getting out of the car and, noting the furious scowl contorting his face, tried without success to choke down the laughter that was bubbling up uncontrollably from inside her. Through the peals of mirth, she asked, "Have you noticed my... face, J. Hollis?"

"No wonder sixth-graders and nineteen-year-olds find you irresistible," Aaron grumbled. He brushed her hands from his shoulders, but trapped one of them in an un-yielding grip and literally pulled her to the doorstep of her condo. Impatience showed itself in his restless shifting as he waited for her to fish her keys from the depths of her tote bag. When she had finally unlocked the door, he scurried her inside with a hand on her elbow, passing though the doorway with her and pulling the door closed behind them.

Judy had regained her composure in the sprint from parking lot to doorstep. "Won't you come in?" she asked, letting a hint of sarcasm drip through her dry delivery.

"Hell, yes, I'm coming in!" he bellowed, and she blinked at him as though he'd lost his mind.

His mind, perhaps, he thought wryly, but not his senses. He was painfully aware of the perfume she wore, of the way her hair would feel if he touched it, the way the sound of her throaty laughter had danced over his senses, arousing them. "I've noticed your face," he said. "The way your eyes flash with emotion, the way you purse your lips when you concentrate, the perfection of your smile. After today, there's nothing I haven't noticed about you." And nothing he'd noticed that he wasn't on fire to explore in taste and touch.

His words stung her with their intensity. She was so unprepared for this, so inexperienced in this type of situation. Panicking because she didn't know what to say, she said the worst possible thing: "A bit hot under the collar, aren't you, Wall Street?"

She had meant it to be light, witty, but it came out as a taunt, a challenge. The sexually raw, dangerous expression in his eyes stole her breath away, and she stood frozen as he stepped closer to her and drew her up in his arms. A gush of air that was part gasp, part sigh rushed from her lips as his fingers combed through her hair and then gently but firmly tilted her head back. She could feel his hot gaze on her face, adoring yet scorching with sensuality, and instinct told her that she had stoked smouldering ashes into fire with her flippant remark.

His lips at first were tentative, testing, but when she did not draw away the kiss became aggressive, and his mouth pressed over hers possessively, branding her with his need. Her lips parted in welcome, receiving him, acknowledging his need and answering it with her own. Her arms hugged him, and her fingers kneaded the hard muscles of his back. With her breasts pressed firmly against his chest, she yearned to be closer still, and the soft layers of fleecy cloth that separated their bodies became a frustration.

Aaron's hard physique pressed into her feminine curves. His lips left her mouth to whisper her name before tracing the line of her jaw to her neck, dropping tiny kisses in their path until he reached the restrictive rib knit of her shirt. With a groan of frustration, he kissed his way back to her mouth and claimed it again, even more decisively than before. His hands slipped down, trailing over her shoulders, then down to the sloping curve of her waist. His fingers slipped under the bottom edge of her shirt and splayed over the warmth of her back, the tips of them following the ripple of her spine and tantalizing the sensitive nerve endings at her waist.

The elasticized waistband of her pants was only a token barrier as he sought more warm, tender flesh and found it in the round swell of her hips. His fingers crushed harder against that precious flesh, and he felt the answering reflexive tightening of her arms around him.

It was the incredible sweetness of her trust that reached him, stopping him when stopping was unthinkable. He forced himself to pull away from her by degrees, his hands sliding from inside her clothes, his lips lifting from hers to press lightly against her temple while he nestled her cheek against his chest.

"J. Hollis?" she whispered—a question, or perhaps a plea. He could feel her trembling and tightened his hold on her. God, what had he almost done?

"Judy, please believe me when I say that I've never wanted to make love to a woman more than I want to make love to you at this moment, but I can't. Don't ask me for explanations, just believe."

Thoughts formed in her mind in disjointed fragments. Disappointment was a living, breathing entity inside her. It was unforgivable that he should draw away from her, inconceivable that he could deliver a pretty little sorry-about-that speech and leave her with every nerve ending in her body calling out for his touch. She'd feared being forced to refuse him, but now she found herself cheated of the opportunity to say yes. What gave him the power—the right—to make her feel this way and then leave her so empty?

And then she remembered "Melissa" scrolled ornately on the title page of the book of poems. She stepped back, forcing his arms from around her. She couldn't take his comfort, didn't want it. "Damn you!" she said, pummeling his chest ineffectually with her fist. "You want everything, don't you?"

He was more startled by her vehemence than by the physical assault. Grabbing her wrists, he thrust his face inches above hers and said, "Don't do this, Judy."

"I should have known better," she thought aloud. "You didn't want me, not when you have Melissa waiting for you up in New England. You just had to prove it to yourself and me that you could make love to me if you wanted to."

His grip on her arms tightened. "Melissa? Where did you learn about Melissa? What did you hear?"

The brusqueness of his voice was a verbal slap in the face. Her fists opened and her arms dropped limply to her sides, pulling her wrists from the circle of his fingers. "The book," she said. "The poetry volume on your bookshelf."

Despondency settled over Aaron, a bleak fog of regret for mistakes past and present, sinister tribute to the mess he'd made of his life. Cupping her chin in his hand, he guided her face up until their eyes met. Her one impression as he looked at her was of sadness.

"Melissa has nothing to do with...she's part of the past."

"Then why?"

Afraid to touch her any longer, afraid even to let himself look in her eyes, he turned away from her. "For a dozen reasons," he said. "Not the least of which is that I wouldn't risk more than the loose change in my pocket on a bet that you're not a virgin."

"I'm not," she said quickly. Then, her voice fading, she added, "Technically."

He emitted a weary sigh. "I would ask you to explain that riddle, but at the moment I'm not strong enough for explanations. All I know is that I've made enough mistakes, and staying here with you would be... dishonorable."

No longer numb, no longer trembling with the shock of loss, Judy was furious, consumed by an anger she couldn't define. "What kind of baloney is that? *Dishonorable*. You sound like the southern patriarch in a Tennessee Williams play."

Aaron turned around. What had ever given him the idea he could bear not touching her? He wrapped his arms around her, encircling her as though he could protect her from harm. That she would melt against him in blind acceptance of his comfort was too much to hope for; it was enough for him that she didn't shrink from him. Lord, but it felt good having her next to him. "You must believe that hurting you is the last thing in the world I'd ever want to do."

He felt her muscles tighten in resolve, saw the gleam of restored pride flash in her eyes. "Look, J. Hollis, things got a little out of hand, and something neither of us wanted to happen almost happened. I'm not some fragile china doll. You don't have to stay here and rub salve on my ego."

Cupping her chin again, he looked directly into her eyes as though he could will her to believe him. "I wanted it to happen, Judy. I still do. And it will."

"I'll be holding my breath with anticipation!" she said snidely. When the ensuing silence grew awkward, she pulled away from him and snapped, "Damned Connecticut Yankees. You don't know when to give up, do you?"

"Now who's playing Tennessee Williams? The classic southern belle?"

"I should have paid attention to my fortune cookie."

"Your fortune cookie didn't say anything about Connecticut Yankees and you know it." How ludicrous it was, how asinine, to be spatting over fortune cookies.

A silence stretched between them, painfully awkward, before Judy said, "Thank you for dinner, Aaron."

He recognized it as a dismissal, just as he recognized that her use of his last name instead of J. Hollis was a gesture meant not to please him but put distance between them.

He stood outside her door feeling like a puppy who'd been exiled from the house after chewing up a favorite slipper. A chuckle rose in his throat, an ugly, self-deprecating, mocking laugh. Judy Harte wouldn't throw a puppy out; she'd give the puppy the other slipper. People were different; she expected decency from them.

Aaron didn't feel decent. Or noble. Or any of the things he should be feeling. God, didn't she know, didn't she sense how difficult it had been for him to let her go? Why couldn't she trust his integrity enough to believe that he had a reason for stopping what he'd begun? He had half a mind to tell her the entire story, and for a few fleeting seconds his hand hovered over the doorbell, ready to ring it. But the half of his mind still left with a modicum of reason stopped him.

What are you going to do, Aaron? Walk in and say, "You're never going to believe this, it's so incredibly funny?" Judy wouldn't see the humor in it. Judy would never speak to him again, once she lashed him open with her razor-sharp tongue and left him to bleed to death.

Ah, yes, I know, he told the internal voice of reason. *Simpson's wife wouldn't be too happy, either.* Judy would tell Gregory, of course, and Gregory would go storming to his mother.

Aaron's feet felt like lead anvils as he walked home. God, how had he gotten mired down in this bog of deception? And why, suddenly, was he so obsessed with Judy Harte?

"You're sure? A one-sided crush?"

"Trust me, Virginia," Aaron said. "I've seen them together. Gregory looks at her like a moon-eyed schoolboy, and Judy tolerates him the way she would one of her infatuated students. She helps him with his physics."

"Maybe he'll pass this semester," Virginia said dryly.

"Gregory may be in for a little heartache when he realizes her feelings toward him are strictly platonic, but he's in no danger of being seduced or coerced into marriage."

"That's a relief," Virginia said, assaulting her salad with renewed interest. "Now all we have to worry about is the money."

Aaron tasted the disappointment as he swallowed a bite of his lunch. "The money?"

"The four hundred dollars. If this girl is so pure of heart, what kind of gift did she accept from him for four hundred dollars?"

"It didn't come up in the conversation," Aaron said. He placed his fork beside his plate with a very deliberate movement and met her eyes levelly. "I want out of this, Virginia. If you have this morbid curiosity, you should go to your son and confront him instead of sending me skulking around behind his back checking up on him."

"If he didn't spend it on her, what did he do with it? And why would he lie when he had no idea I'd hear the story anyway?"

Aaron exhaled an impatient, exasperated sigh. "There are hundreds of reasons a young man Gregory's age might need some extra cash. Maybe he got into a poker game."

"Or got some girl pregnant?" Virginia said, cocking an eyebrow.

"He might have had a fender bender and not wanted to file an insurance claim, or maybe he loaned a friend some money. Let it alone, Virginia. If it's anything earth-shattering, you'll find out about it sooner or later. And if it's something minor, it's not worth worrying about."

"If it were a girl ... in trouble, I mean, do you think we could definitely rule out this Judy Harte? Maybe she had a boyfriend who ducked out on her and he's loaning her the money."

"Judy? Certainly not. She's not the kind of woman ... she's too smart to let herself ... it's just impossible, that's all."

"I see," Virginia said, forcing the phrase to sound vague and noncommittal, but something in her look seemed to be suspicious of Aaron's exuberant defense of the girl. She stretched her hand across the table and clasped his forearm. "You will keep trying to find out about the money, won't you?"

"Virginia," he said, exasperated.

"It's not spying anymore," Virginia said. "I'm not asking you to...purposely involve yourself with this Harte woman or my son any further. It's not like I'm asking you to *romance* her anymore." She bit the inside of her lip to keep from smiling. "But now that you know her and Gregory, it wouldn't hurt for you to just...keep your ears open. Just in case."

"I'm not promising anything."

"Of course not. And if we never discuss this topic again, I'll understand perfectly. Now I'm afraid I have to eat and run. I've got a dozen last-minute errands to run this afternoon. We're flying to the Poconos for Thanksgiving, you know."

"Trace mentioned it."

"I'd much rather go at Thanksgiving than Christmas. Among other things, I don't have to bother cooking a stupid turkey. Let Trace's sister do that! I think I'll call your mother while I'm there. Maybe she can meet me at Macy's for some early Christmas shopping."

Aaron grinned. "All you'll have to do is mention shopping, and she'll be there with her credit cards at the ready."

"I'll tell her you sent your love."

Chapter Six

Judy looked out her bedroom window to discover, for the thousandth or perhaps ten-thousandth time, why she loved living in Florida. Thanksgiving Day, and it was sunny and mild. Cobalt-blue skies were feathered by fluffy white clouds, and the temperature hovered just under seventy degrees—cool enough to make the heat from the turkey-filled oven seem cozy but not uncomfortable, yet not cold enough to necessitate the hassle of coats and mufflers. A perfect day for a long, leisurely walk after the traditional feast, Judy mused as she idly stared at the small lake that had added several thousand dollars to the price of each unit in the complex.

A solitary figure at water's edge caught her eye, and she was startled to recognize the lonely silhouette as J. Hollis. Intrigued, she stood at the window and studied him as she might study a work of art in an effort to discover nuances of shading. He was wearing snug-fitting jeans and an athletic gray fleece shirt, and his hands were tucked into his

back pockets as he stared at the water or, perhaps, his reflection on the water's surface. What was he doing all
alone on a major holiday?

*He just moved here, dummy, and he doesn't have fam-
ily nearby,* she thought. Still, it was incredible that a man
like J. Hollis Aaron had no one to spend Thanksgiving
with. Surely he had *something* planned.

That's not the stance of a man with plans, her mind argued. His was the posture of a man without plans, a man
feeling as abysmally alone as he appeared to be, staring at
his own reflection in a lake. Abruptly she lowered the mini-
blinds on the window and dashed down the hall to the
closet where she stored Fluffy's leash. "Fluffy!" she
called. "Here, Fluffy. Come on, girl. We've got a rescue
mission."

Fluffy showed up, wagging her tail so enthusiastically
that her entire body vibrated, making it difficult to fasten
the hook of the leash on her collar. "Hold still," Judy
prompted. "Wanta go see J. Hollis? Yeah. J. Hollis. Remember? The man with the doggie biscuits. Whataya
think—turnabout is fair play?"

Aaron was skipping stones across the water's surface,
and with that peculiar concentration of his was oblivious
to her approach as he watched the stone's path mark the
smooth water. J. Hollis Aaron, she mused idly, would not
make a good sentry if he was preoccupied.

He was stunningly virile in the casual clothes with the
breeze gently tousling his hair, and Judy took advantage
of his preoccupation to catch her breath and organize her
thoughts.

"You do that very well. They must have lakes in Connecticut," she said.

Absently wiping his gritty palms on the rough denim of
his jeans, Aaron turned, feeling as though he'd been

caught doing something illicit and at the same time afraid that he'd imagined her voice because he needed so badly to hear it. Finding her there was a relief as well as a joy. She was casually but elegantly dressed in charcoal-gray slacks and an oversized aqua sweater that made her eyes appear even greener than usual. Opaque stockings, black kid flats and a long strand of large *faux* pearls quietly completed the understatement. He'd never seen her more lovely, never wanted so badly to touch her.

"With luck, the lake on the estate will be just right for ice-skating by next month," he said. Then, bobbing his chin at Fluffy, he observed, "She's heeling nicely."

"Yes," Judy said. "She's very intelligent."

Did she know how seductive her unconscious gesture of chewing on her bottom lip was? he wondered, and decided she didn't. If she knew, he mused, she would stop it immediately. Whatever she was trying to do at the moment, it *wasn't* to seduce him.

"I saw you from my window," she said, her eyes aimed somewhere at his chest, avoiding direct contact with his. Aaron nodded but didn't comment.

Judy took a deep breath, shifted her weight from one foot to the other and stared down at the leather loop on the leash in her hands as if making sure it had not slipped away from her. This time she forced herself to look at his face, and when she spoke it was with a gush of words that spilled out of her in one long, continuous sentence. "I know you don't know many people here yet, and it doesn't look as though you have any plans for today, and it seems a shame since it's Thanksgiving and you should be with people, and I have an aunt with a table that seats eight and only five expected for dinner, and I know she wouldn't mind if I brought you along since besides my uncle there may not be any men there and my aunt misses her sons, and besides all that she's like a mother hen who loves to have a brood of chicks under wing anyway, so Fluffy and I wondered if you wanted to go to my aunt's for turkey.'' The exhausted sigh that followed seemed a perfectly appropriate and inevitable accompaniment to this remarkable speech.

Aaron was too addled by the combination of her unexpected appearance, the unorthodox invitation and the stunning vision she was with the morning sunlight dancing in her hair to reply immediately.

''Well?'' she prompted finally, cocking her head expectantly.

A devilish twinkle sparked in Aaron's blue eyes. ''That was certainly a very eloquent invitation.''

With a delectable pout forming on her mouth, Judy planted balled fists at her waist. ''But?''

''But I'm sure your aunt wouldn't appreciate you dragging a stranger to Thanksgiving dinner unannounced.''

''Well, she's my aunt, and I know she wouldn't mind one whit if I brought a friend along.''

''A friend?'' he said, cocking an eyebrow.

Judy bit the inside of her mouth to refrain from picking up the gauntlet. She'd come to rescue him, not fight with him. She had delivered the invitation; now there was nothing to do but wait for his response. She waited. And waited, while his eyes roved impudently over her face and then languorously ravished the rest of her, making her feel as though wearing clothes had been an exercise in futility. How dare he? How dare he, when she had come extending the hand of kindness and friendship? ''*Just* friends,'' she said irritably. ''That's a stipulation.''

Aaron wasn't at all sure he wanted to be taken to her aunt's house like a wet kitten rescued from a rainstorm, but he was quite positive that he wanted to be anywhere in the world that allowed him to be close to Judy Harte for as

long as he could wangle it. "I would love to have turkey at
your aunt's," he said, "but I insist on changing clothes."

Judy returned his smile. "Fluffy and I are going to make
one lap around the lake. I'll meet you in the parking lot in
twenty minutes."

Aaron almost danced back to his condo. Who would
have believed it? After enduring a week of her trying to
avoid him and being politely remote when she was forced
to acknowledge his existence on Planet Earth, Aaron had
actually been invited to a family dinner by Judy Harte. If
he were in search of a miracle to give thanks for on this
Thanksgiving Day, this would be it!

Twenty minutes was not a generous amount of time in
which to dress, but it hardly necessitated the haste with
which he shaved, slapped on after-shave and changed
clothes. He was driven by a sense of urgency, an impatience to be with her. It took, by his watch, thirteen minutes before he was dressed and groomed and another two
for him to select an appropriate wine from the bottles
stored on the portable rack in his pantry.

It was only when he was on his way out the door that he
remembered he had to call Jack Sawyer. Fishing his address book from his portfolio, he found the number and
dialed. "Jack? Hello. This is Aaron.... Actually, yes.
That's what I'm calling about. Would you be heart-
broken if I bowed out this evening?"

He laughed into the receiver. "A better offer? You might
say that." He laughed again, a smug, conspiratorial chortle of the kind he'd share in a locker room. "She's a heck
of a lot better-looking than you are and not nearly as
married as your wife. Um-hum, I plan to do just that.
Yeah ... A rain check? Sure. I'll come for turkey tetrazzini tomorrow night. You guys have a nice one, too. And
leave enough turkey for the tetrazzini."

* * *

Judy's aunt and uncle lived in a stucco ranch home nestled on a three-acre tract in Kissimmee, just south of Orlando. The front yard was tropically landscaped with a variety of palms, elephant ears and lush shrubbery. Behind the house there was a small stand of citrus trees heavily laden with fruit.

"We call that the orchard the way your folks call their place the estate," Judy told Aaron as they walked up the long sidewalk to the front door. It had been a companionable drive, and they had chatted comfortably about the weather, the scenery—which had ranged from freeway to seedy nightspots to country roads—and Judy's Aunt Martha and Uncle Brad.

"Uncle Brad's retired air force," Judy had told him. "They spent his last four years at Fort Patrick and just stayed in Florida when he got out. Ronnie's a year older than I am and is in the air force now, stationed in Germany, and Liz is two years younger than I am. She lives in Tampa, but she'll be there today with her kids—Kevin, who's four, and Amy, just three months old."

After pausing thoughtfully, she had added, "Liz and her husband split up just before the baby was born, and she's ... well, she's not adjusting too well. Aunt Martha warned me not to mention Sam. I thought I should explain so you won't go putting your foot in your mouth, either. Liz was always crazy about him."

"It's amazing what people who are supposed to care about each other do to each other," Aaron said thoughtfully. "I mean, it seems to start out happy enough, and then one day..."

"Their marriage didn't fail in a day," Judy said. "All the stresses got to them gradually, I guess—jobs, kids, mortgages." She paused. "Then Sam got involved with a woman at his office." Her eyes blazed with an unexpected vehemence. "It was unforgivable. Liz was pregnant with his child, and he was out . . ."

"You're right," Aaron said flatly, before she had a chance to transfer her hostility from Sam to all men, including him. "It was unforgivable."

"Needless to say, he's persona non grata in the Harte family."

"The Harte family? So this uncle is your father's brother?"

"Um-hum. If you knew my father, you'd see the family resemblance immediately. They're almost like twins."

It was Uncle Brad who answered the door, greeting Judy with a bear hug and Aaron with a firm handshake. "Is that Judy?" a woman's voice queried from a distant room.

"Sure is," Brad called to his wife. "And she's brought a young man. I think you'll like him—he's carrying a bottle of Rhine wine."

"Sounds like my kind of man, all right," called a voice from far away. "Bring him to the kitchen, Judy. I'm kind of involved in here."

Martha looked up from forming bread dough into cloverleaf rolls when Judy and Aaron entered the kitchen. "You'll forgive me for not shaking hands," she said cheerfully, waving fingertips shiny with melted butter in the air for their perusal. Aaron thought idly that he hadn't seen a bibbed apron with starched ruffles since the last episode of *Leave it to Beaver*. Even his mother had switched to canvas butchers' aprons with clever captions.

"Good grief!" Martha exclaimed, catching sight of Fluffy. "That can't be the same puppy."

"Oh, but it is!" Laughing, Judy slid the casserole she was holding onto the counter. "Here are the sweet potatoes. You know when to put them in the oven. Aunt

Martha, this is my neighbor, J. Hollis Aaron—*J* the initial, not Jay like the bird. He just moved here from New York."

"It's nice to meet you, Mrs. Harte," Aaron said, putting the bottle of wine next to the casserole. "I hope I'm not intruding on a family occasion."

"Certainly not, J—was it Harry?"

"Hollis," he said. "It's my mother's maiden name."

"Oh, how lovely. Well, we're delighted to have you with us. You don't by any chance carve, do you?"

Judy giggled. "His father's a surgeon."

"The job's yours," Martha said.

Still laughing, Judy put her hand on Aaron's arm. "No one in the Harte family likes to carve the turkey, especially Uncle Brad. And with Sam—" Her laughter instantly dissolved. "Oh, damn! Where *is* Liz? I saw her car out front."

Aunt Martha sighed and heaved her shoulders in a weary shrug. "She's upstairs feeding the baby."

"How is she?"

Martha stared at the dough she was working. "She's smiling, but not with her eyes." Her fingers flew back to work, busily tearing off a piece of dough, rolling it in butter, fussily positioning it in the pan. She looked from Judy to Aaron and back. "Kevin's out in the Florida room with his toys. Why don't you go say hi."

"I was just about to take Fluffy out there, anyway," Judy said. "Are you sure there's nothing I can do to help in here?"

"If J. Hollis is going to carve the turkey for us, that's help enough."

"You do know how to carve a turkey, don't you?" Judy asked on the way to the porch.

She might as well have been Bacall asking Bogart, "You do know how to whistle, don't you?" Aaron had to suppress a strong urge to nibble at the alluring smile that had settled on her lips or drown in the scent of her perfume by nuzzling her beautiful neck. He was forced to settle for grinning down at her. "I didn't inherit my father's propensity for scalpels, but I can handle a carving knife adequately."

"I'll just bet you can," Judy said under her breath. Quickly she reached for the knob of the door that opened onto the screened Florida room, grateful for something benign on which to focus her attention. Light banter couldn't mask the undercurrent of sexual tension that had been flowing between them ever since she'd found him earlier in the day. It was a volatile current, deceptively subdued at times, then blazing hot during unexpected moments. It had flared when he'd looked at her so boldly at the water's edge, and it flared again just now when their teasing words had borne no resemblance to the actual communication taking place.

His hand casually cupped her elbow, sparking memories of other times, other touches. Remembered sensations rippled through her body, her mind, her soul.

How had she been naive enough to think they could just leap into a platonic friendship after impassioned kisses and a fiery confrontation had left her emotions shattered and confused? She'd thought he was the vulnerable one when she'd spied him so alone beside the lake; now she realized it was she who was vulnerable. It wasn't friendship she wanted from him, not relief from the stilted awkwardness of the cold war they waged when they happened to meet in the courtyard or at the spa. It was...

She didn't know. She didn't know what perverse motivation had inspired the insanity that led to her inviting him to a cozy family holiday gathering, but she did know that she was relieved he'd agreed to come with her. And she also knew that—despite the bitter aftertaste of the ugly scene they'd played in her living room and the fact that as a Treadmill Clone, his entire philosophy of life was diametrically opposed to her own—she wished they were alone so he could kiss her the way his eyes were saying he wanted to kiss her.

Her little cousin, dressed in denim coveralls, had mapped out a miniature highway on the floor and was so totally involved in coordinating the complex maneuvers of a caravan of metal trucks that he did not look up as they came in. Judy was glad he didn't acknowledge their arrival immediately because it gave her a few seconds to pull in the reins on her besieged emotions. It was a hell of a shock to be standing in the home of beloved relatives on Thanksgiving Day, watching a dear child drive toy trucks over an imaginary highway, and suddenly face the indisputable fact that she was falling in love with a man she scarcely knew and didn't entirely trust.

Chapter Seven

Measured with a ruler, it would have registered only a fraction of an inch—the distance Judy moved toward Aaron as they stood there watching Kevin play. But in that minute space there existed a commitment, an acceptance of that new development in her life. What it meant, where it would lead, Judy didn't know. It was simply a fact.

As if sensing the significance of her nearly imperceptible movement, Aaron stretched his arm across her back and kneaded the ball of her shoulder with his hand. She became aware at once of his warmth and of his strength. And that she would be content to remain within the reach of his touch for the rest of her life.

"Ju-deee," Kevin said, finally noticing her arrival. Then, seeing Fluffy, he said even more exuberantly, "Fluffy!" In a dash he was across the porch, throwing his arms around the dog's neck and burrowing his face in her fur. Fluffy's name gurgled from his throat again amid giggles of pure delight.

Judy gave him a few seconds with the dog before saying, "Hey, Kevin. How about me? Do I get a hug, too?"

The child's ambivalence was amusing to behold. Half of him clearly wanted to let go of Fluffy and give his special cousin a hug, but the other half of him just as clearly wanted to get on with the business of rough-and-tumbling with the dog. When Judy knelt and opened her arms, however, he dutifully stepped into them and allowed himself to be hugged.

"How's my favorite fellow?" Judy asked.

Noting the affection in her voice, the beatific expression on her face as Kevin patted her back with his small hand, Aaron experienced a piercing stab of jealousy. *Her favorite fellow, indeed!* Instantly he was ashamed of his pettiness. It was unreasonable to be jealous of a four-year-old child. *But then,* he thought wryly, *reason was not a quality he associated with his feelings for Judy Harte.* There seemed to be no moderation in him where she was concerned. She had a way of brewing emotional storms in him that threw his responses off-kilter; her acerb wit pushed buttons that set off alternating explosions of fury and passion inside him.

He tried to garner some enthusiasm as Judy introduced him to Kevin, but felt awkward. Children always made him feel awkward because they were an unknown quantity to him. With them, he had no points of reference, no younger siblings, nieces or nephews. They were a nebulous gray area into which other people journeyed, normal people who fell in love, became a couple and wanted two point three kids and a house in the suburbs.

Kevin regarded him with round, serious eyes. Oh, Lord, Aaron thought, what am I supposed to do? Surely the kid wouldn't want a hug. Tentatively, feeling a fool, Aaron extended his hand as he would upon meeting a business acquaintance. To his utter surprise Kevin grinned, said, "Gimme five!" and slapped it.

I'll be damned, Aaron thought, disconcerted to find himself thinking that the little tyke was kind of cute. He had large, twinkling brown eyes, small even teeth and a cherubic flush to his smooth cheeks. His hair was curly and thick like Judy's—a family trait that appeared to be passed on from generation to generation. Her Uncle Brad's hair, despite a salting of gray, remained thick and curly.

Aaron thought of his mother and the grandchildren she waited for so futilely. Was this what the yearning was all about, the preservation of family traits, the reassuring perpetuation of a bloodline? Aaron knew she felt cheated because she'd been able to have only one child, that she was depending on him, as her sole heir, to compensate her by filling her life with young ones. Then she could finally spill the cup that ran over with the hugs and kisses and unquestioning love she hadn't managed to use up when he was growing up. It was a grave responsibility and, Aaron had always thought, one that had been thrust upon his shoulders unfairly.

Was that why he'd allowed himself to get so involved with Melissa, a woman who was very straightforward about not wanting children who would interfere with her career? Was that one of the things that had drawn him into an engagement fatally inflicted with that disease known as apathy? The irony of his mother's bitter tears upon hearing that the marriage was off still intrigued him. He'd kept Melissa's no-children stipulation secret from her to protect her from disappointment, and when he'd called off the wedding, his mother had wept as though the precious grandbabies she'd anticipated had been wrenched from her arms by brute force. It would have been funny if it hadn't been so tragic. He would have told her all about it if he'd thought she'd appreciate the black humor, but he was certain she would have found the truth even more depressing than what she'd perceived as the truth.

So he'd gone south, leaving his ex-fiancée and his grandchildless mother to sort out the mess he'd seemed to make of their lives. He'd tried to ignore the mess he'd made of his own, but his disillusionment and unhappiness just grew worse. Then he'd met Judy, and for a time it had seemed he was destined to wreak havoc in her life, too. But today there was hope for forgiveness, renewal, a new beginning.

An honest beginning. Of what? Of normalcy, he hoped. Of freedom from commitments he did not want and of freedom to make commitments he chose. It was why he'd left New York—not running away from his mistakes, but running to a chance to amend his way of doing things so he wouldn't keep making the same mistakes over and over.

A loud peal of childish laughter cut through the serenity of the porch with the startling impact of a wailing siren, and Aaron was jerked from deep thought. Kevin was lying on the floor being assaulted by wet kisses from Fluffy.

"What's all this noise in here?" Kevin's mom, infant in arms, had stepped onto the porch.

"Fluffy likes me!" Kevin squealed.

"I think it's a mutual attraction," Judy said with a laugh.

"I'd say so," Liz agreed with a chuckle. "Gosh, that puppy has grown."

Judy put her hand on Aaron's bicep. "You can introduce yourself, I believe. Liz, give me that baby before I burst." As Liz settled the baby in Judy's waiting arms, Judy cooed at it, "Hi, Amy. How's Mommy been treating you?" Leaving Aaron and Liz to finish getting acquainted, she settled into a wicker love seat and continued talking to the baby.

"You'd never know she was the genius of the family, would you?" Liz said affectionately. "She's absolutely bonkers over kids." Turning to Aaron, she extended a baby-lotion-scented hand. "I'm Liz, Judy's cousin."

Aaron shook her hand and smiled. "I'm J. Hollis Aaron, her neighbor." She was taller than Judy, he noted, with high cheekbones that lent her a cool, classic beauty. Her thick hair was lightened to a pale blond and sleeked into a ribboned ponytail at her nape. Her blue eyes held a slightly haunted look.

Fallout from her broken marriage, Aaron thought. He wondered fleetingly if broken engagements put the same expression in a woman's eyes, but quickly suppressed the guilt that would engulf him if he let it.

While Liz answered a summons from Kevin to say hello to Fluffy, Aaron sidestepped boy, mother, dog and toy trucks to reach the wicker love seat where Judy was seated. "Mind if I sit down?" he asked.

"Amy and I would be delighted to have you join us," she said, smiling. When Aaron was settled beside her, she nodded toward the baby. "Isn't she terrific?" She pressed her forefinger into the center of the baby's palm, and Amy's tiny fingers closed around it. "Look at her perfect little hands."

"She's awfully little," Aaron said, shifting uncomfortably.

"You should have seen her when she was born, all tiny and wrinkled. She's a big girl now." Giving Amy an impulsive hug, Judy said, "And you're still growing, aren't you, Amy? I wouldn't be surprised if you had a tooth by Christmas. What do you think, J. Hollis? A tooth by Christmas?"

Judy shifted her gaze from Amy to Aaron, expecting some response from him. What she saw was incredible. A blush was crawling up his neck. She watched, mesmerized, as it crept upward to stain his cheeks. There was something akin to terror in his eyes.

"I don't know," he said. "Is she old enough to have teeth?"

Judy burst into laughter. "If I weren't holding Amy I'd hug you, J. Hollis. You don't know *anything* about children, do you?"

"Not much," he admitted, wishing she wasn't holding Amy. There was a pause before he said, "You like kids, don't you?"

He'd asked the question for the sake of conversation, yet it didn't sound like casual conversation. It didn't *feel* like a casual question as it passed through his vocal cords. He found himself holding his breath as he waited for her answer.

"I love 'em." The simple sentence, the statement of a fact that was easily observable, reeked with significance. *I want children of my own,* it said.

They were like birds in a bizarre courtship ritual, Aaron thought, dancing in circles around their individual needs and goals, not yet ready to discuss them or acknowledge their readiness for compromise, not yet ready to admit that their individual needs and goals could be interrelated. *Damn!* he thought, clenching his jaw. He wasn't prepared for this; it was too soon, too close in time to the fiasco he'd left behind him.

"Would you like to hold her?"

Aaron blinked at her. If he'd thought she was trying to instill a love of children in him so that he would want children of his own, he'd have wrung her neck. But she wasn't manipulating him. In fact, he wasn't even certain she was aware of the dance they were doing. Perhaps he was over-reacting; children were, to him, a sensitive subject.

"I don't think . . ." he said, but she waved aside his refusal with her free hand.

"Come on, J. Hollis. Babies like to be held by men. They sense strength, and it makes them feel secure."

"But I don't know how."

She laughed. "You've got all the equipment."

Amy was a pink-clad bundle of warmth when Judy plopped her in his lap. Immediately she screwed up her face, preparing herself to release a wail of protest. At the first whimper, Aaron cast Judy a desperate look that said, "What do I do?"

"Bounce her a little," Judy instructed. "Just be sure to keep your arm behind her neck. See."

Indeed, it seemed that the crisis was averted. Amy's face straightened, and when Judy leaned over to touch her nose and coo, the baby even smiled. Aaron watched while Judy continued making faces and uttering inane remarks, inciting Amy to full, gurgling laughter.

Why was it, Aaron wondered, that everyone assumes that anyone with any sense wants to *hold* a baby? Most of his friends were married, and many of them had children. And he'd never visited one of them with a little present of some sort without being asked if he wanted to *hold* the baby. For thirty-two years he'd managed to avoid that singular privilege.

And then he'd met Judy Harte.

He became aware of a peculiar sensation on the top knuckle of his forefinger, and discovered that Amy found it very appetizing. She was gumming it wetly. He tried pulling it away, but the tiny child proved to be a bundle of strength and persistence, gripping his finger firmly and following his hand as he drew it away. "Is this safe?" he asked Judy.

Judy grinned impishly. "For you or Amy?"

"For Amy," he said tersely.

"Have you had your rabies shot this year?" Judy asked. Then, reading the irritation mounting on Aaron's face, she bit the inside of her bottom lip to check her own smile. "It's probably a sign she's getting that Christmas tooth."

Judy's uncle had installed a chime box on the porch so that if someone rang the front doorbell it could be heard. The unexpected jangle from the small box startled Fluffy, who ceased her playing to yip ferociously at the air, and Amy let go of Aaron's finger abruptly to put her mouth into position for a full-fledged cry of indignant protest at all the racket. Aaron began bouncing her frantically to quiet her while Judy stroked the child's head and murmured reassurances. Kevin, now on all fours, began barking in unison with the dog.

"I wonder who that is," Liz yelled over the din. "Mother and Daddy aren't expecting anyone else."

A muffled masculine dialogue started in the distance and moved closer until words were distinguishable. "I have a right," of indeterminate origin, followed by Brad Harte's voice saying, "At least let me prepare..." were as plain as day. A tall man in casual slacks and a sweater stepped onto the porch and stopped so abruptly at the sight of Liz that Brad Harte stumbled into him from behind. Martha Harte appeared in the doorway on her husband's heels and, wiping her hands on a terry dishcloth, took in the mayhem in one panoramic sweep of the room.

The baby was still crying despite Aaron and Judy's earnest efforts to quiet her, Fluffy and Kevin were barking, Uncle Brad was fuming and Aunt Martha's gentle gray eyes were filled with panic.

"Liz," the tall man said.

Liz had stood up and was staring at him. "Sam."

For a moment no one moved. Then Fluffy bounded across the room to sniff the newcomer's ankles and Kevin raised himself up on his knees. "Daddy!" he yelled, and getting up as quickly as possible he ran to the welcome of his father's arms.

"This is quite a surprise," Liz said to Sam.

"I...Thanksgiving," Sam said sheepishly. "I just wanted—"

"I'm sure there's room for another plate," Liz said, giving her mother a look that said undeniably, "I want him to stay."

"Y-yes. Of course, Sam. Of course you're welcome to join us," Martha said. Brad exhaled heavily, and his tense shoulders slowly returned to their relaxed posture.

Judy took Amy—who appeared to be the only one who didn't realize the crisis was past—from Aaron's arms, and rocked the baby against her shoulder. "Welcome to a nice, quiet Harte family Thanksgiving," she whispered to Aaron. "I thought *Liz* looked haggard, but Sam's lost twenty pounds, at least."

With a shake of her head, Aunt Martha turned toward the kitchen. Uncle Brad remained in the doorway, leaning against the jamb with a studied casualness while he warily eyed his estranged son-in-law. Sam gave Kevin a bear hug, holding on to the child as though his life depended on it. Finally, when Kevin grew impatient with the affection, Sam swatted him lovingly on the bottom and lowered him to the floor. "There's a couple of surprises on the back seat of the car," he said. "Why don't you go get them."

"I'll walk with him and help him carry them in," Brad said, taking his grandson's hand.

Judy had managed to reduce Amy's temper display from a full-fledged squall to an occasional whimper. One pitiful whimper drew Sam's attention the way a snapping twig does a wild animal's. His head jerked in the direction of the cry, and he said in an anguished voice, "Amy?"

He stalked across the room in large strides, accidentally kicking one of Kevin's metal trucks into a skid in his haste. He stopped short in front of Judy and stared at the baby, his baby daughter, with eyes that were at once filled with sadness and awe. He said her name again, with the reverence of an astronaut stepping onto a distant planet. "Amy."

Judy held the baby up so that Sam could take her. He became oblivious to everything else as he held his daughter in his arms and repeated her name as he studied her smooth little face and perfect tiny hands. Finally his eyes sought out Liz. "She's grown so much."

"Babies do that," Liz snapped, but the sharpness of her reply was tempered by the tenderness visible on her face as she looked at Amy nestled in Sam's arms.

Kevin returned carrying a cardboard carton by the built-in handle, and a pink plush toy bunny. He walked straight to his mother and thrust the bunny into her hands. "This is for Amy."

"It's pretty," she said, looking past the toy at Sam. Her eyes met with her husband's and locked there for a moment before she turned back to Kevin. "What have you got, sweetheart?"

"Fire truck," Kevin said, holding the box so she could see the illustration.

"That's super," Liz said.

"I can put it together all by myself."

"I'm sure you can."

Uncle Brad had been standing just inside the doorway, witness to the intimate exchange between his daughter and son-in-law. A scowl momentarily passed over his face, but he quickly disguised it. "Why don't you come with me into the living room, Kevin. You can put it together in there while we watch football."

"Can Fluffy come, too?" Kevin said. Obviously it was a condition of his going.

"Oh, sure, why not?" Uncle Brad said. Then, with a raised eyebrow at Judy: "As long as she sits down and behaves."

"She will," Judy said. "Just tell her to sit."

Casting another glance toward Amy and Liz, Brad shifted restlessly, as though making a tough decision. "Judy, you and J. Hollis might want to watch the game, too, Miami's playing."

They took the hint and followed Brad into the house, leaving Sam and Liz alone with the baby. Judy touched Aaron's arm to stop him as they passed the kitchen door. "I think Aunt Martha could use a hand with the last-minute details. You don't mind if I volunteer, do you?"

He brushed a lock of hair away from her cheek, and his eyes swept over her face. "Of course not. I was planning on becoming a Miami fan sooner or later."

"I guess now's as good a time as any."

He kissed her forehead. "I guess so."

"Keep an eye on Fluffy. I'd hate for her to get thrown out in disgrace."

"Sure," he said, and kissed her once more before leaving.

Aunt Martha was basting the turkey when Judy approached. "One of these years I'm going to try those bags that do the basting for you," she said.

Judy laughed. "I'll believe that when I see it. They've had those bags for years and years and you haven't switched yet!"

Finished, Martha closed the oven. "It just wouldn't seem the same."

"Without the love?" Judy teased.

Martha chuckled. "You're a joy, Judy. You always were. You and I have always been on the same wavelength, haven't we?"

"I'd like to think so," Judy said. "It's a nice wavelength." Martha's kitchen always made Judy feel at home, welcome. She went to the sink and began washing the romaine lettuce Martha had set out. "Caesar salad again?"

"Thanksgiving, Christmas and Easter. No surprises."

"We, uh, got one today, didn't we?" Judy said, nodding toward the Florida room.

"Some people did, I guess," Martha answered cryptically.

Judy cut off the water, dropped the lettuce in the sink and looked at her aunt. "You knew he was coming?"

Lifting the edge of a cotton dish towel to check on the progress of the dough rising in the muffin pans, Martha said, "I didn't know. But I wasn't surprised." Her shoulders sagged as she sighed. "Sam's been a member of this family six years, and he hung around here a couple of years before that. I feel about him almost the way I do about my own blood kin. When I found out about . . . what he was doing, I could have loaded up Brad's old shotgun and let him have it for the way he hurt Liz, Kevin and Amy. But you know, Judy, I couldn't bring myself to hate him. I couldn't hold on to the anger long enough—love kept getting in the way. And I couldn't fault him any more than I would one of my natural children for doing something stupid."

She turned to face Judy and leaned casually against the counter the way Judy had seen her lean against it countless times before. "That's what it was, you know. It was wrong, of course, but he's not a bad boy. It was just a stupid mistake. I figured he'd realize that sooner or later. From the looks of him, I'd say that's exactly what he's done."

With a shuddering sigh, she wiped her hand over her face. "I just hope Liz is smart enough to see it the same way."

"You mean you *want* Liz to—"

"Open your eyes, Judy. Those two have always been crazy about one another. They've got years of experience and two kids in common. Liz would be a fool to throw it away over pride."

Judy didn't try to resist the urge to hug her aunt. "I feel exactly the same way, but I chalked it up to being a hopeless romantic."

Martha harrumphed and stepped out of Judy's arms as though she'd had enough sentimental nonsense. "Hopeless romantic, indeed. Maybe that's your excuse. Just seems like common sense to me that two people who care about each other and have two beautiful children should be together."

"You're a fraud and you know it." The words were spoken with affection. Martha pointedly ignored her, and Judy went back to washing the lettuce.

A few minutes later, Martha said, "There's nothing else to be done except wait for the turkey to finish cooking. Why don't we go sit a spell? I want to get to know that young man of yours."

"My *neighbor*," Judy corrected. "I spied him standing all alone at the edge of the lake and felt sorry for him."

"He sure must be a grateful type of fellow," Aunt Martha said, deadpan. "I saw him kiss you twice right out in the hall."

For a split second their eyes met, and then they burst into giggles like a pair of schoolgirls.

In the living room, Martha took one look at her husband, planted her fist on her waist and shook her head in exasperation. Uncle Brad was stretched out in his favorite recliner, snoring softly. "I don't believe it!" she said. "I'm sorry, J. Hollis. I'll have to apologize for sleepyhead's rudeness. To hear him tell it, he's the nation's biggest football fan, but he hasn't made it to the first-quarter bell in the past ten years. Football works faster on him than Valium. Please don't be offended. It's not the company."

J. Hollis laughed softly. "No offense taken. My father does exactly the same thing on those rare occasions he actually gets as far as sitting down in front of the set."

Kevin, who was seated on the couch next to J. Hollis, held up the instruction sheet that had come with his building set. "What do I do next, Aaron?"

The unexpected camaraderie that had apparently developed between the two fascinated Judy, and she watched spellbound as J. Hollis studied the illustration and then pointed out the blocks Kevin needed next for the fire truck. Kevin listened with intense concentration as Aaron pointed to the picture and explained where the next blocks would fit. Then, when he'd picked up the blocks, he thrust his chin in the air and said, "I'm doing it all by myself. He's just showing me how."

Judy and her Aunt Martha exchanged glances, and both had to bite back laughter over the child's precocious display of independence. When it was apparent neither of them was going to comment, Aaron said, "He's doing a good job."

Judy could have hugged him for saying it. Praise was exactly what Kevin needed, what the moment called for, and Aaron had provided it succinctly. She *would* hug him, she decided, at the earliest opportunity. Her slight smile told him that from across the room.

Martha dropped into the bentwood rocker across from the couch. "Why don't you come show Grandma how much you've gotten done," she said to Kevin. "I haven't had enough time with my big boy today."

The child went willingly, climbing into her ample lap to be circled by loving arms while she listened patiently to every word of his detailed account of fitting the blocks together.

Aaron was aware that Judy had settled onto the couch beside him. He reached for her hand and held it loosely in his own to acknowledge and welcome her presence. But his attention was focused on Kevin and his grandmother and the comfortable rapport the two shared. This was what his mother wanted—a grandchild to cherish and nurture, a tiny being of her own lineage to climb into her lap and be loved for its very existence. He'd always thought it an obsession with her, a slightly perverse determination to find something in life she'd been denied that she could zero in on and yearn for so her life wouldn't be stigmatized by perfection. Perfection, everyone knew, was boring.

She and his father would be entertaining or entertained today, he knew. They would have planned an intimate meal with close friends—turkey, or a pheasant perhaps, with the proper appetizers and wines and something cold and flavored with expensive liqueur and topped with heavy cream that would prompt comments about cholesterol and calories and make everyone feel deliciously indulgent for partaking. It would be cold and snowing, and there would be a roaring wood fire in a stone fireplace. And Maxine

Hollis Aaron, elegantly understated in tweed slacks, an oxford shirt, a Shetland sweater and solid-gold earrings, would idly comment that holidays would somehow have more meaning when her restless son settled down and there were little ones around.

For the first time, Aaron perceived his mother's attitude as more sad than irritating. He'd been too busy resenting the unwanted responsibility she was heaping on his shoulders to consider that her desire for grandchildren might be a perfectly natural phenomenon, that she might feel as guilty about saddling him with a mission he found impossible to fulfill as he felt over not being able to provide what she asked. She was, after all, of a generation that had been taught such expectations were reasonable. Perhaps his decision to remain unencumbered by a wife and family seemed as radical and unfair to her as her expectations did to him.

Kevin finished the fire truck, and after tolerating a hug and praise from his grandmother, climbed down to test-drive the vehicle across the floor. His realistic sound effects jerked his grandfather to wakefulness. Shaking the cobwebs of sleep from his brain, Brad looked around the room and asked, "What's the score?"

Martha harrumphed in disapproval, but Aaron said evenly, "Still ten to seven."

"What quarter is it?"

"Still the third," Aaron said.

"Then I must not have missed much," Brad said. A beat of silence was followed by a round of rollicking laughter.

It felt good to laugh, Aaron thought. And good to have Judy's hand in his. He gave it a squeeze and smiled at her when she turned her face toward him and cocked an eyebrow as if to ask what he'd meant by the gesture. He felt a lump of well-being form in his chest and grow until he thought he might burst trying to contain it. What would her uncle and aunt think, he wondered, if he pulled her next to him and gave her a bear hug for no reason at all except that it seemed like the most natural thing in the world to do?

"I finished my truck," Kevin said.

"Let me see," Brad said.

"I'm going to show Daddy," Kevin announced, after Brad had given it the requisite inspection and seal of approval and given it back to his grandson.

Alarm showed in Martha's eyes, but her voice when she spoke was even. "Why don't you show him later, Kevin. He and your mother are talking right now."

"But he wants to see it," Kevin argued.

"How would you like to take Fluffy for a walk?" Judy asked. "You can hold the leash."

Kevin cocked his head and considered his options. "Take Fluffy for a walk?"

"Sure," Judy said. "J. Hollis and I will go with you. I wanted to show him the orchard, anyway."

Martha pulled herself from the rocker. "I'll get you some bags. You can pick some fruit. You have relatives up north you could ship them to, don't you, J. Hollis?"

"I couldn't . . ." J. Hollis began, but Judy and Martha both waved away his protest.

"Pick a couple of dozen or so," Martha said. "We've got a bumper crop this year."

"Might as well resign yourself to going home with some fresh fruit," Judy told him. "It's a family tradition."

"But I'm not fam—"

"You're here, aren't you?" Martha snapped. "That makes you honorary family for the day."

"Give up, J. Hollis," Judy said with a peal of laughter. "No one ever wins an argument with Aunt Martha."

Outside, Kevin and Fluffy dashed ahead of the adults. "If Fluffy weren't so well behaved now she'd be dragging Kevin instead of running along with him," Aaron said.

"Is that an I-told-you-so?"

He gave her a sideways glance and grinned. "There may be a small element of I-told-you-so. Mainly it was an observation."

"I suppose I deserve it. I do appreciate your helping me with her. I'd never had a dog before, and I hated having to discipline her."

"I'll bet you don't have any qualms about disciplining your students."

"If sixth-graders aren't disciplined, total anarchy prevails."

"You're a braver soul than I am to spend your day surrounded by smart-mouthed kids."

"You don't like kids much, do you?" She felt his hesitation as she waited for an answer. It was as if he was looking for the right words to express himself.

"You didn't know much about training dogs; I don't know much about kids."

"You did all right with Kevin," she said.

"He was sort of cute, with that fire truck and all."

"Yes." Her eyes wandered to the porch where Sam, still cradling the baby in his arms, and Liz were just ill-defined silhouettes through the screen walls. "Sam certainly knew what he would like, didn't he?"

Aaron followed the direction of her gaze. "Do you think it's significant that he showed up today?"

She turned to face Aaron. "It could be the first step toward a reconciliation."

"After what he did?"

"He was so pitiful, J. Hollis…so thin and haggard. And did you see the way he looked at Amy? If that didn't reach Liz, nothing will."

"You're of the forget-and-forgive school?" he asked.

She paused thoughtfully and finally said, "It depends on the situation, what's involved. In their case, it's a marriage and two small children."

They were silent until they reached the small grove and Aaron, sticking his hands in the back pockets of his corduroy jeans, surveyed the profusion of ripening fruit weighting the branches of the carefully pruned trees, and said, "Now I feel like I'm in Florida."

Judy's laughter tinkled with crystalline crispness in the clean air. "I reacted the same way the first time I came here. It was a shock after the bitter winters in Massachusetts."

"Is that where you're from originally?" he asked, becoming engaged in a tug of war with an orange.

When he emerged victorious, Judy opened a brown grocery bag. "You'll get the knack of it," she said. "And no, I'm not from Massachusetts. I'm from Williamsburg, Virginia."

Aaron plucked a second orange and carefully lowered it into the bag. "So what were you doing in Massachusetts? Teaching?"

"Going to school. I was working on a graduate degree at the Massachusetts Institute of Technology."

"Really?"

She sensed the subtle change in his attitude while he looked at her as though appraising her. No, she thought with a stab of resentment. Not appraising, reappraising. Of course a Yalie would respect a good school, a northern school. He would have a new respect for her, not for having studied there but for having been accepted to study there. From his perspective, being admitted to M.I.T. would be ever so much more impressive than teaching public school in Florida.

"Pick some more oranges," she said sharply.

"Yes, ma'am," he said, feeling somehow rebuked and not knowing why.

"I don't see Kevin and Fluffy," Judy said, setting the bag on the ground. "I'd better make sure they're okay."

"Find them?" he asked when she returned.

"Yes, on the garden swing. They were so cute. Kevin was so small in that big seat, and Fluffy was spread out next to him with her chin on his knees and they were rocking, and Kevin was chattering away. I would love to have eavesdropped, but I was afraid he'd see me and it would spoil the moment."

Her smile was genuine, her voice warm with the tenderness she felt toward the child. That tenderness reached out to Aaron, drawing him to her with a startling ferocity. One long step brought him close enough to hold her, and he gathered her into his arms and hugged her fiercely. Surprised, she started to speak, but he captured the comment, still unspoken, as he claimed her mouth in a kiss that was urgent and probing.

After raising his lips from hers, he remained aware of the rhythmic movement of her breasts against his chest as she breathed. Her lips were lushly bruised by his ardor, her eyelids gently closed, her cheeks flushed. She clung to him as though she feared she might crumple to the ground if she didn't have him to hold on to.

"God, Judy, what you do to me," he said, squeezing her in his arms as though he could obliterate their clothing and fuse their two identities into a single entity. "Do you know? Do you feel it, too?"

"Yes," she said, the word a fragile puff of air.

"The force of it scares me to death," he said, tracing the lines of her ear with his finger.

"And me," she whispered. She could have put a name on it, this terrifying force, but she wasn't sure he was ready yet to deal with a concept as formidable as love.

Chapter Eight

They parted gradually—the loosening of the embrace, the withdrawal of an arm, the last reluctant relinquishment of the contact that was so precious to them both. The ensuing silence was long and absolute, until Sam's agitated voice carried across the lawn from the porch. "But I love you, dammit! All of you."

Judy and Aaron looked at each other, slightly embarrassed to have heard the plaintive plea meant only for Liz. Judy grinned. "What he lacks in eloquence he makes up in sincerity."

"He did sound as though he meant it," Aaron said.

"Desperately," she said.

A thoughtful frown creased Aaron's forehead and dragged his mouth. "Women have a way of making men desperate." He exhaled a weary sigh. "I suppose it's been that way since the beginning of mankind."

"This looks about full," Judy said, referring to the bag of oranges. "Shall we switch to the tangerines?"

Later, after they'd put their bags of harvested fruit in the car and gone back to the house, Judy left Aaron and Kevin in the living room and went directly to the kitchen to help with the last-minute details of the meal.

The covered roasting pan with the turkey in it was sitting on a cushion of pot holders on the countertop, a pot of green beans was simmering on a back burner and Aunt Martha was stirring the base she was browning for gravy. "Your sweet potatoes are in the oven along with the rolls," she told Judy.

"What can I do?"

"Lordy, I don't know what to tell you to do first. I guess you could put ice in the glasses. And you could dig through that drawer with all the spatulas and cooking spoons in it and see if you can come up with the corkscrew. I'd get Liz in here to help, but I'm not sure we ought to disturb them. They've been having a rather spirited discussion. Lord knows I don't want to go out on that porch and disturb them."

"Why don't we send someone a little younger?" Judy suggested. "Someone . . . oh, about thirty inches tall."

Martha ceased her stirring and stared at her niece. "That's absolutely devious, Judith Harte." Then, with a wink, she added, "I don't know why I didn't think of it myself. We'll send Kevin as soon as the food's on the table. Let's just hope this meal's not so awkward that we all die of indigestion."

She needn't have worried. Sam and Liz made their entrance at the peak of the turkey-carving, wine-uncorking, getting-everything-settled confusion. Liz's eyes were red-rimmed from crying, but no one commented, just as no one commented on the despair that made Sam's face appear older than his thirty years. When everyone was seated, they slipped into comfortable patterns developed over years of togetherness. Sam was a part of the family, as he had been for many years.

Following grace, the Hartes observed a unique Thanksgiving tradition. Each person at the table would mention a few of the things he was most grateful for before they drank a toast to health and prosperity. Uncle Brad began. "I am grateful for health, for prosperity and for a wonderful wife. I am thankful that we could all be here together. And of course I am especially thankful for Amy, who joined the family this year."

Everyone chuckled and looked at Amy, who was sound asleep in her infant seat and blissfully oblivious to the celebration going on around her. Judy was next. "I'm grateful for health and prosperity and loved ones and Amy and Fluffy and the freedom to invite a *special* friend to share Thanksgiving with people I love." Feeling Aaron's perusal from across the table, she wondered if he'd heard the intonation she'd purposely given the word special. His enigmatic smile and the glint of pleasure in his eyes led her to believe he had.

"You're welcome to participate if you'd like to, J. Hollis," Brad said when Aunt Martha had said her piece and Aaron was next in line.

Judy held her breath, hoping he wouldn't be embarrassed or feel as though he'd been put on the spot. But he appeared to be perfectly at ease as he said, "I am grateful for a new home, new beginnings and the start of new friendships."

Judy swelled with pride for him, for his equanimity and poise and his ability to be at home with strangers. But then why should she be surprised at his social prowess, his confidence? Because, she realized suddenly, although she was in love with him and felt she knew him in a way that was fundamental and instinctive, he was still new to her—they were new to each other. If their relationship developed further, they had a long journey of discovery ahead of them.

Her concentration was interrupted by Kevin's recitation. He named his grandparents and Fluffy and his mother, then concluded, "And I'm glad my daddy came and brought me a fire truck."

"From the mouths of babes," Martha whispered under her breath, and a shroud of silence settled over the table as everyone waited to hear what Sam would say.

Sam shifted uncomfortably as a blush of emotion spread over his face. His voice was crackly and weak, as though it had passed through a parched throat from a great distance. "I'm grateful . . . for Amy, who wasn't with us last year." He paused to lick his lips. "And I am grateful to be here with people who mean…people who are dear to me."

Everyone shared the misery of his self-loathing, his utter defeat. Even Kevin seemed to sense the unrest in the poignant statement and said, "Daddy?"

"It's all right, Kevin," his father said, putting his hand on top of the child's as it rested on the tabletop. After a space of time that seemed infinitesimal, Liz reached out for her husband's other hand and wrapped hers around it. Sam looked at her questioningly, found a message of affirmation in her eyes and then threaded his fingers through hers.

"Is anyone else hungry?" Liz asked pertly. "This all smells delicious. Daddy, make the toast."

"To health, prosperity and loved ones." Glasses were raised, and the simple toast was repeated en masse.

"I want a turkey leg," Kevin announced before the glasses were even returned to the table.

"You're in luck," Martha said, passing the platter of turkey to Aaron. "We've got two of them, and only one kid old enough to eat them." She chuckled. "If I can ever get all my grandkids here at once, I'll have to make two turkeys so we'll have enough drumsticks."

"Your son and his family are in Germany?"

She nodded. "They've been over there eighteen months this tour."

"Ronnie is career air force like Uncle Brad," Judy said. "This is his second tour overseas."

"He goes every chance he gets," Brad said. "We did, too."

"We're going to visit them next fall," Martha said. "Brad likes to take in *Oktoberfest*, and I enjoy just watching the leaves turn colors. As much as I love Florida, I miss the distinct change of seasons."

"How long have you been here?" Aaron asked.

"Close to eight years," Martha replied. "Brad's last four years were at Fort Patrick, and we've been in Kissimmee ever since. We'd just moved into this house when the doctor sent Judy south to recuperate."

Aaron looked askance at Judy. "Recuperate?"

Judy dismissed the question with a wave of her hand. "Aunt Martha exaggerates. I had a cold I couldn't shake, and it was a bad winter in Massachusetts, so—"

"She had a severe case of pneumonia brought on by exhaustion. She looked half-dead when she got off the plane. The only reason the doctor authorized travel was to get her out of that wretched cold. If she'd stayed there another week she'd have been dead."

"Translation: it was a rough semester and I'd been hitting the books pretty hard and I was a little pale," Judy said.

"You were utterly exhausted, physically and mentally," Martha said.

"Are you and Judy having a fight?" Kevin asked his grandmother, enchanted by the prospect.

"Judy's having a little trouble remembering," Martha said. "I'm reminding her how she wound up in Florida."

"All that matters is that she came and she stayed and we're glad," Brad said. "My brother was a little disappointed that she never went back to finish her thesis, but quite frankly my brother can be an ass at times."

"Brad!" Martha exclaimed, "What kind of way is that to talk about your brother in front of Kevin?"

"You have a brother?" Kevin asked.

"Your Great-Uncle Mark," Liz said.

"I'm a brother now, because Momma went to the hospital and got Amy." He sounded more enamored of the idea of being a brother than of having a sister. Stealing a glance at Judy, Aaron noted that she was having a tough time containing a grin.

"You were working on your master's thesis?" he asked.

"Master's, hell! She was a semester away from a Ph.D.," Brad said.

Martha directed a censuring glare at her husband. "Brad! Your language."

"I know about hell," Kevin volunteered. "The preacher says that's where bad people go."

"A Ph.D.?" Aaron said. "At M.I.T.? In what?"

"Physics," Judy replied unenthusiastically.

"You were a semester away from a Ph.D. in physics from M.I.T.?" Aaron said incredulously.

"She was on the list for an astronaut slot," Brad said.

"Along with a few thousand others," Judy said.

"A few hundred," Brad corrected. "She'd made the preliminary cut."

"Are you going to be an astronaut, Judy?" Kevin said.

"No," Judy said, frowning slightly. "Although your Great-Uncle Mark used to hope so."

"Is Great-Uncle Mark really a donkey?" the child asked.

"A donkey?"

"Grandpa said—"

"We all know what Grandpa said," Martha said. "And he just meant that Great-Uncle Mark is a little stubborn at times." Poking her fork in her dressing deliberately, she added, "It's a Harte family trait."

"I wish you could be an astronaut, Judy. Then you could bring me a piece of the moon."

"What if I built you a rocket instead?"

"Could you do that?"

"I not only could do it, I will. And we'll launch it and watch it fly way, way up until we can't see it, and then the parachute will open and we'll have to go chase it."

Kevin's eyes were round as silver dollars. "Promise?"

"Cross my heart," Judy said, drawing an imaginary X on her chest.

"Do you wear those kind like they show on TV?" he said.

"Those kind of what?" Judy asked.

"Those kind of cross-your-hearts that lift and separate."

He watched as the adults gasped collectively and then, one by one, burst into laughter.

"What's so funny?" he asked.

"You watch too much television," his mother said sharply.

Kevin shook his head as though they'd just confirmed his premise that all adults were dumb.

"Do these stacks look about equitable?" Judy asked,

referring to the fruit she'd divided into four piles on the top of her breakfast-nook table.

Aaron was leaning casually against the wall with his arms folded across his waist. He eyed the piles of citrus critically. "Maybe you should count them to make sure we get the same number," he suggested, a boyish grin betraying his intended humor.

Judy picked up an orange and dropped it gingerly into a brown grocery bag. "One." She picked up another. "Two."

Aaron burst out laughing. "I wasn't serious."

"No?"

"No, and you know it." He stepped behind her and looped his arms around her waist. She dropped the handful of fruit into the bag and leaned her shoulders against his chest. For a while neither of them moved or spoke, and the silence between them was a comfortable one.

"All in all, it wasn't a bad Thanksgiving," Judy mused, enjoying the warm solidity of Aaron's body.

"It was a wonderful Thanksgiving. Judy..."

"Hum?" she said, languidly.

"I'm glad you asked me."

"Are you? It was kind of chaotic, with Sam showing up and Kevin's unexpected comedy routine."

"Kevin's a smart little kid," he said, still slightly mystified to find that he actually thought so. *I'll be damned,* he thought, *the little rapscallion actually charmed me.*

"Precocious is the word," Judy said. Aaron's cheek, with half-a-day's growth of beard, was rough as it pressed against the softness of hers.

Another silence, one mellow with their closeness, stretched between them, and when Aaron spoke his voice was husky with sensuality. "You're wearing that perfume again. Allure, isn't it?"

Judy didn't want to move, didn't want to step away from his strength or give up the delicious little nibbling kisses he was pressing on her temple. The seductive warmth of his body was having a drugging effect on her senses and her sense, and she knew, even as she sighed languidly and allowed her body to meld even more intimately against his, that she had to draw away from him before she lost the faculty of reason altogether. None of the issues that had ripped them apart the last time they were close had been resolved. She might have fallen in love with him, but she hadn't lost her mind. She wasn't ready to trust him, or her judgment where he was concerned.

"Judy?" he said, sensing her withdrawal. "I'm not ready for today to be over." He hugged her a little tighter and emphasized his words with intensity. "I don't want to let you go."

He felt the muscles in her cheek move as she smiled. "Friends," she said, knowing what she asked was impossible but hoping for a compromise. "It was a condition."

"Then let's just talk." Reluctantly he took his arms from around her as if to prove his earnestness—and felt a stabbing loss as she drew her body away from his.

She turned to face him. "Talking might be . . . we need to talk." The pain of the ugly scene at their last meeting twisted through her chest as her eyes met his unflinchingly. "It's time you told me about Melissa."

A frown distorted the aesthetic perfection of his face. "There's nothing—"

"If you tell me it's none of my business, I'll accept that," she said. "But if it's none of my business, then we don't have anything at all to discuss."

He understood her implicitly. It was time for trust, the shedding of secrets. Melissa was ensconced irrevocably in his past, but Judy didn't know that. He owed her that knowledge if he expected her to be a part of his present.

And your future? a voice inside him nagged. *Aren't you deceiving yourself into believing you can separate the present from the future?*

It hasn't come to that yet, he argued with himself.

Are you sure? Is Judy making the same distinction between present and future?

The future hasn't been mentioned.

You hurt Melissa—do you want to hurt Judy, too?

No. But I won't just walk out without giving it a chance.

Giving what a chance?

The future.

Oh, God, he thought, suddenly desperate with realization. When had it happened? He hadn't meant for it to happen.

"Aaron?"

He blinked himself back from the netherworld of thought. "I'm sorry. Did you say something?"

"Just that the house is on fire, the sky is falling and there's a wild tiger loose in the living room."

He winced. "Was I that far away?"

"It would seem so. Would you like coffee or something?"

"Maybe later," he said.

So, she thought, we're going to talk.

They squared off at opposite ends of the sofa. Judy kicked off her shoes and tucked her legs up under her as she leaned against the plump corner pillows. She looked, Aaron thought, tiny and adorable, and the couch suddenly seemed ridiculously long and she was intolerably far away. What was she doing so far away when he wanted so badly to be touching her?

"Melissa and I were engaged," he began abruptly. "We were supposed to get married in September, but we didn't."

"Why?" Judy asked hoarsely, despising the morbid curiosity that was causing her to pry so mercilessly into his personal life. "You don't have to tell me," she said quickly. All she'd really needed to know was that he was not committed to someone else while he was wanting to make love to her.

"I think I do," he said. "I don't want you imagining that I left New York because of some shattering experience that broke my heart. You're not going to make a tragic hero of me, Judy. I don't deserve it. I'm not noble enough for heroism. I was the one who canceled the wedding."

He had peeled away the veneer of suavity and confidence to show her the guilt and self-loathing consuming him under the surface, and Judy found the intimate new knowledge of him disconcerting, as though she'd asked him to take off his shirt and been forced to examine unsightly scars he would have preferred to keep hidden.

Relinquishing the lush softness of the corner pillows, she moved to the center of the couch and caressed his cheek with her fingertips. "You're more noble than you think," she said.

He lifted his hand to capture hers and brought her fingertips to his lips and kissed them, one by one. "I'm not noble at all."

"You must have had a good reason to end it," she said.

"I should never have let it begin. It just sort of...evolved, and I let it go on because it *should* have been right—two attractive, successful people with so much in common. We dated. We became lovers. Marriage seemed like a logical progression of events. We bought rings, and then we ordered wedding invitations, and then we went shopping for a refrigerator.''

He guided her fingers to his lips again and held them there, but he seemed to her to be far away again, as though he were telling the story to a distant audience—a jury, perhaps, appointed to condemn or vindicate him according to how well he presented his case.

"It fell apart very abruptly. We were in the middle of the store and Melissa told me how important it was that we get the right kind because we'd have to live with whatever we bought for so long. She started asking me questions, demanding decisions. Did we want an ice dispenser in the door? A digital clock? Side-by-side or traditional? White or almond?''

After planting a kiss on the inside of Judy's palm, he clasped it to his chest as he would a precious thing. She felt the rhythmic rise and fall of his chest as he breathed.

"Have you seen the bumper sticker that says 'The one who dies with the most toys wins?'" he asked, and she nodded. "That's the way it was. I found myself wondering if she expected to be given a higher berth in heaven if she had a digital clock on the refrigerator door when she died. I lost track of what she was saying, and finally she put her hand on my arm and said, 'Aaron, you're not paying attention,' and I said, 'Frankly, my dear, I don't give a damn.'"

He paused as though he were considering nuances of the situation he'd never examined before. "If she had laughed, I probably would have married her. But she just stared at me as though I'd lost my mind. We fought that afternoon and all through dinner, and she stormed out of my apartment that night.''

His chortle of laughter was flecked with bitterness. "She left in a huff, but she wasn't in too much of a hurry to remember her Reeboks and her Sony Walkman."

Judy yielded to the temptation presented by his broad chest and nestled her cheek against it, stretching her arm around his waist. "Was that the last time you saw her?"

"It should have been. I wish it had been. But it was so petty an issue; it didn't seem *significant* enough to break up an engagement. No, we kept trying to patch it up, but the rifts just got bigger and bigger. After a week I realized there wasn't enough plaster in the world to fill in the holes and cracks in our relationship, and I told her I wanted to call it off."

He drew a ragged breath. "Melissa isn't the type to tolerate defeat, so when our engagement *failed* . . . well, she saw it as my failure, not hers. She was hurt and very bitter. She said I had a total inability to handle commitment." Though Judy couldn't see his face, she sensed his frown. "Maybe she was right. I certainly couldn't handle that one."

"It would have been the wrong commitment for you to make," Judy said, lifting her head from his chest to look at him.

His face surrendered itself to a tender smile as he cradled her chin in his hand. "You're sweet, Judy. I wonder if you know how seductive your sweetness is."

Say something! he thought. *Protect yourself from me.* But she remained perfectly still, as if poised for his kiss, and the invitation of her slightly parted lips was irresistible. For a sliver of time, the mere seconds that it took for him to close the distance between them, the innate innocence about her made him feel like the Big Bad Wolf in pursuit of Little Red Riding Hood. How could he talk to her about another woman and then kiss her so cavalierly?

He found it surprisingly easy. Kissing her was perhaps the easiest thing he'd ever done. But letting her go—letting her go proved impossible. Her sweetness filled him, thrilled him, intoxicated him. He could end the kiss, but he was incapable of relinquishing the ecstasy of having her body touching his. He held her in his arms, a warm bundle of sweetness and womanhood. Her breasts were firm and round against his chest, her waist tiny under the span of his hand, her full hip solid where it brushed his thigh.

It was more than physical. Physical he'd had—with Melissa. And before her... with the Manhattan pediatrician and the advertising executive and the college professor. This was more. It went beyond the physical into the realm of the spiritual. This woman cuddled in his arms understood him better than any human being on the face of the earth. He knew it with an intuition that was intangible yet unquestionable. By some mysterious, involuntary force they were totally involved with one another. They had not yet become lovers, but already they were closer than friends of many years.

Realization and acceptance came to him in one thunderbolt to the mind—this was the element that had been missing with Melissa, with all the other women in his past. He had been seeking it without knowing what it was he sought.

His left arm tightened his hold on her, anchoring her next to him, where she belonged, where he needed her. He lifted her left hand in his right hand. It was so small compared to his. With his strength he could crush it with little effort, but he would die before he would hurt her. It amazed him to remember that he'd found her brash when he'd first met her, mistaking her wit and quickness of tongue for toughness. She was not tough. Strong, perhaps, but also tender and, in her sweetness, vulnerable.

He kissed the top of her hand and tasted her skin briefly with his tongue. "I'm not supposed to be doing this, am I?" he said.

She grinned at him haughtily. "You have a rather extreme method of proving yourself friendly."

He laughed aloud and hugged her reflexively in a gesture of pure delight. And then he kissed her again, and joy metamorphosed into a need that was white-hot and undeniable. It was easy, far too easy, to shift her in his arms and ease her back onto the couch and stretch out full-length beside her, luxuriating in the warm softness of her.

The swell of one breast pressed tightly against his chest. His hand sought her other breast and cupped it through the bulky knit of her sweater. A deep rumble of desire rose in his throat, emerging as a sensual growl when she gasped and then sighed contentedly in response to his bold touch and pressed closer to him. His mouth lowered over hers urgently, plundering her sweetness. One of her hands combed through his hair while the other kneaded his shoulders.

His mind, his body, the very essence of him zeroed in on his need to possess her. Bending his knee, he draped his leg across hers in a mindless quest to be as close to her as humanly possible. His hand slid down her side from her breast to the curve of her waist and over the swell of her hip as he searched for the bottom of her sweater.

Judy was adrift in a sea of churning sensation, lost but not caring that she was lost. His touch was magic, the response it evoked in her enchantment. The voice of logic warned her to stop, but she ignored it, wanting conversely for his spell never to stop weaving its magic around her. This was the love sung by balladeers, the passion that inspired poets. His body was next to hers, lean and strong, and his mouth was hard upon hers, his lips teasing, his tongue titillating. And she loved him, loved the sensations he stirred in her.

The masculine coarseness of his hair abraded her fingers tantalizingly as she combed them through its thickness, and the sinews of his shoulder muscles begged for her caress. She had never felt anything so splendid as those hard muscles, never felt so much a woman as she did when confronted with the stark reality of his manhood.

His hand was warm on her breast, searing her with delight through the knit of her sweater, and the heat of his caress followed his hand down over her ribs and hips. His thigh moved over hers, heavy and warm with a fire she'd never experienced, and she instinctively arched her body closer to his, drawn by the fire.

His hand was closer now, inside her sweater, his fingers rocking her sea of sensation with the kneading of her full hips. The scent of his after-shave surrounded her while she nibbled at the tender flesh behind his ear, hungry for the taste of him as his hand pushed higher inside her sweater, searching for the plump ripeness of her breast.

Abruptly his hand ceased its movement, and she felt herself being lifted slightly from the couch before his hand moved again, hardly an inch, and then stopped. The curse he mumbled under his breath surprised her enough to allow logic a toehold in her passion-muddled mind. He was fighting with the bottom rib of her sweater, unable to raise it without her conscious cooperation.

She would have cooperated, gladly, enthusiastically, if Fluffy hadn't chosen that exact inopportune moment to demand attention, leaping onto the couch and landing unsteadily with two paws on each of them. Aaron repeated the curse he'd mumbled earlier, loudly and with verve, as the dog fought to stabilize her footing and succeeded only in gouging toenails into flesh.

The sheer absurdity of the situation struck Judy as hilarious, and the intensity of a different emotion still close to the surface caused her to overreact. Swinging her arm ineffectually at Fluffy to push her to the floor, she burst out laughing.

Aaron managed to sit up and shoo the dog down much the way he might have an overwrought turkey. "Damned mutt!" he said. Then, turning his full attention to Judy, who was still laughing hysterically, he said, "I don't suppose I'd have much luck kissing you right now."

Still hysterical, she put her hands on Aaron's shoulder and shook her head. Trying to swallow her laughter, she said between gulps, "I'm sor—sorry. It's... just... Fluffy... and..."

Aaron leaped off the couch and stood with his back to her. The utter desolation in the set of his shoulders sobered her instantly, and she stood up and lightly placed her hand on the small of his back. "J. Hollis?"

He spun around, and the frustrated fury in his eyes burned through her and the vehemence in his words stung her. "Pardon my ego, but I'm not used to being laughed at in the middle of making love."

"I wasn't laughing at you," she said. "I was laughing at—" Her eyes widened, and her mouth flew open. She closed it with a gulp. When she spoke, her voice was hoarse with awe. "Did you say we were making love?"

"I certainly thought so. It was more than a casual grope to me."

"Oh, J. Hollis," she said, and he couldn't read the emotion that tinged her voice with breathlessness.

All the frustration of the interrupted interlude welled up inside him, and he lashed out at her. "Why can't you call me Aaron like everybody else?"

"Why don't you have a name instead of an *identity*?"

"I do have a name, dammit. It's Aaron."

Her fingers brushed over his cheek as their eyes met and locked. "I'll call you Aaron, if you like."

Sighing wearily, he put his arms around her and threaded his fingers through her hair, holding her head against his cheek. "I want you, Judy. I'm trembling with the physical need for you. Let's go to the bedroom, close the door and make love."

"This isn't supposed to be happening," she said. "We were supposed to be friends today."

"Friends make the best lovers."

He was stunned when she pulled away from him, shocked and rendered helpless by the unpredictable withdrawal. He mutely witnessed the tremor that racked her shoulders, and didn't know what to do. The bitterness of her words was more shocking still. "I'm so smart," she said, "So damned intelligent. A certified genius." Slowly she turned and lifted tear-filled eyes to his. "I don't know a damned thing about lovers."

Aaron's heart melted. He felt it expanding, spreading like a puddle of warm wax waiting for her to do with it as she pleased, for now it belonged to her. He opened his arms in an instinctive gesture of comfort, and she ran into them and clung to him like a frightened child. God, why hadn't he realized—hadn't he known she was innocent? Hadn't he asked her if she was a virgin? And she'd answered with a riddle. Lord, what did he know about dealing with virgins? How long had it been since he'd encountered one in a romantic context? High school? College?

Relying on instinct, he kissed her temple and stroked her hair and spoke soothingly to her until he sensed that she was calm. Several silent moments later, he said, "What did you mean about not being a virgin—technically?"

Very gently she extracted herself from his embrace. "Let's take Fluffy for a walk around the lake."

When they reached the shore of the lake, she gazed up at the moon. "It should be cold," she said. "On a November night, we should be greeted by a shock of cold air instead of this compassionate temperateness."

He agreed. A shock of cold air might have been almost as good as the cold shower he desperately needed.

There was a park bench at the far side of the lake, and they sat down. The water was dark except for the reflection of the moon and stars on its still surface. A host of unseen frogs croaked a discordant serenade. The vaccination tag on Fluffy's collar clinked as the dog sniffed unfamiliar night scents in the grass.

"You think I'm a virgin," Judy said. "I'm not."

No reply seemed apropos. Aaron threaded his fingers through hers and waited for her to continue.

"It's hard to imagine what it's like being a child genius if you haven't lived it," she said. "We were a special, segregated little group—the eggheads, the brains. Normalcy was considered very unoriginal and oh-so-uncreative, so most of us weren't very normal. It was a peer thing, to see who could be wittiest and who could pull the most bizarre stunts. One of the boys showed up at the senior prom driving a hearse, that sort of thing. We spoke a different language from the other kids because we weren't kids at all. We were brains riding around in teenage bodies."

Aaron spread his arm across the back of the bench, and Judy leaned her head against it. "We were so smart, so sophisticated. And there wasn't a lick of common sense divided among us. We were intellectual giants and social imbeciles. I started college at seventeen, and I might as well have been twelve. You know what it's like being a college freshman. Everyone was trying everything they hadn't tried before—cigarettes, drugs, philosophies, sex. I'd never felt the least urge to smoke cigarettes, and drugs didn't hold any fascination for me. Neither did all the wacky cults I could have joined."

She sighed and smiled sadly at him as their eyes met. "To be honest with you, I wasn't exactly raging with unfulfilled desire, either. I was too naive. But enough guys had asked, and I'd heard as many girls relate their tales of blissful deflowerment that I became curious about sex."

She sighed gently. "And began wondering if I were a normal candidate for womanhood. So when the boy I was dating told me he wanted to make a woman of me on my eighteenth birthday, I agreed. He arranged for his roommates to be out all night, and I lost my virtue on a cord bedspread in a dorm room while someone down the hall was playing the school fight song over and over on the stereo."

She shook her head sadly. "I never went out with him again. I woke up the next morning a little sore and feeling—" she shrugged "—I don't know, empty. Exploited. But I didn't feel like a child who'd become a woman through some magical process. I didn't feel any different at all."

Resting her neck against the cushion of his biceps, she tilted her head back and closed her eyes. "I wasn't curious anymore. Sex was no big deal. It was just one more thing that had been hyped out of proportion by television and movies."

Opening her eyes, she caught Aaron studying her face. She lifted her head and smiled. "That was years ago. Eventually I realized that everything about that night was wrong, and that the partner I chose and the reason I agreed were the wrongest things about it. And I decided that next time it would be with the right person for the right reasons, and that it would be very special.''

Pure, unadulterated desire blazed in his eyes as he traced the curve of her cheek with his forefinger. "I want to make love with you, Judy."

Her hand covered his, and she smoothed her cheek against his palm, then met his eyes unflinchingly. "I know. And I know that it's only a matter of time, and that when you do it will be very special."

Aaron silently congratulated himself on his clumsiness and stupidity. "I promise you it won't be impromptu on the sofa with a dog providing comedy relief," he said gravely.

Her cheek gravitated naturally to the beckoning cradle of his shoulder. "In my fantasies I never imagined it the way it was tonight. I guess every woman wants to dream of an elegant dress and candlelight and soft music. But if it had happened tonight, my only regret would have been our lack of responsibility. I wouldn't have enjoyed spending the next couple of weeks sweating out whether or not we were going to be dealing with an issue we might not be ready for."

He knew what was coming before she said it, and he steeled himself. Still, the ramifications hit him like a physical blow to the guts when she said, "I'm not protected."

"And I didn't ask."

"I wonder...." she said, and her voice faded.

"What?" he said.

She waited a long time before answering. "I wasn't stopping you," she said. "It was so...special, Aaron. It was magic for me. I couldn't think about anything except you when I was feeling that way. I was just wondering if...whether...if there was a chance...."

He cupped her chin in his hand and tilted her face so that he could see it, and smiled at her tenderly. "This is the first time I've ever heard you tongue-tied. What is it you're wondering?"

"If it was just a little bit special for you." God, what was she doing asking him for reassurance like an adolescent? *Dumb, dumb, dumb!* she chided herself, and began chattering nervously before he could answer. "You're older than I am, Aaron, and I know you're ... that you've been with other women, and—"

"Judy," he said, hugging her shoulders, and she was aware of his face moving toward hers, slowly, deliberately. "Judy, it was more than a *little* special for me." And then, in that last fragment of time before his lips touched hers, he whispered, "It was ..."

The rest of his remark was drowned in the sweet urgency of a kiss.

Chapter Nine

Answering the unexpected ring of her doorbell, Judy opened the door to a colorful bouquet of cut flowers thrust forward by the hand of J. Hollis Aaron. "Good morning," he said.

"Good morning," she said, stepping aside so he could come in. She was delighted, surprised, relieved to see him.

"I just happened to have the day off, and it occurred to me that you have the day off, too, and it seemed a pity to waste such a beautiful day being apart when we could be enjoying it together. Wherever you want to go, whatever you want to do, I'm at your disposal."

Judy giggled. "Does that include voyages through the solar system in a starship?"

"Who said the sky had to be the limit?" he said flamboyantly.

"There's a new show at the planetarium. But the museum doesn't open until noon."

Aaron consulted his watch. "That gives us a little over two hours. Are you hungry? I skipped breakfast."

"The museum's in a park. We could pack a picnic."

There was a playfully lecherous tilt in the lift of Aaron's eyebrows. "A loaf of bread, a jug of wine and..."

"Turkey sandwiches from the turkey Aunt Martha sent home with us," Judy finished. "I've got the loaf of bread and soft drinks. I doubt if they would allow wine in the park, anyway."

"We'll drink from our imaginations."

"My, but you're waxing poetic today."

"Your beauty brings out the poetry in my soul."

And your eyes bring out the fire in my blood when they touch me that way, she thought. He was giving her the romance she dreamed of, the subtle seduction of flowers and poetry. This tender generosity was a nuance of his personality she'd never seen before, and it filled her with sadness to think that it might be merely an extension of his treadmill personality to want to do anything he did right, whether it was an investment package or a seduction. *Oh, Aaron, while you're seducing me couldn't you fall just a little in love with me?*

It didn't take them long to make sandwiches and load Judy's picnic basket with the pantry potluck.

"Planning on an orgy?" Aaron asked as Judy put a generous cluster of grapes into a plastic bag.

"In the middle of a public park?" she asked. "That wouldn't do much for your professional credibility."

"There's more to life than credibility," he said, wrapping his arms around her waist from behind and brushing her hair off her neck with his chin, nuzzling it. "That perfume is enough to incite an orgy—or is it just the way it smells on you that drives me crazy?"

I wish I knew, she thought. *I wish I could be sure I'm special to you and not just convenient.*

The mail truck was pulling out of the parking lot when they passed through the courtyard, so they stopped to check their mailboxes. "I've got to get Gregory's mail, too," Judy said. "He asked me to pick it up for him while he's out of town so his box wouldn't get crammed too full."

"Let's hope he got something more exciting than a credit card bill," Aaron said, frowning at the one he'd found in his box.

"Or a sales brochure," Judy said, holding up a slick circular advertising a private pre-Christmas sale at a department store. "It's a good thing you and I have charge accounts. Otherwise neither of us would get any mail."

She unlocked Gregory's box and peeped inside. "Doesn't look as though Gregory fared much better," she said, reaching for the solitary envelope. "This is strange," she said, staring at the letter after she'd pulled it from the box.

"What?" Aaron asked, alerted by the change in her tone of voice.

"This letter's addressed to me in care of Gregory. Why would anyone send something to me in care of Gregory?"

Aaron read the return address. "American Kennel Club."

"*Kennel* Club? Do you think it could have something to do with Fluffy?"

"I thought you said Fluffy was a mutt."

"She is."

"Judy, the A.K.C. is *the* kennel club. They provide registration papers for all the breeds. But they wouldn't be contacting you about a mutt."

"Do you think I should open it?"

"It's addressed to you."

She ripped open the envelope. "What . . . it's papers for a—what's this, briard?—named Judith's Fluffy Heart-song Joy."

"Of course!" Aaron said. "A briard. I always thought Fluffy's markings were familiar. You've got yourself a show dog, lady."

"But Gregory said—"

"How did Gregory get involved in this?"

"Fluffy was a birthday present from Gregory. He asked what I wanted and I said a puppy, and he asked what kind and I said just some hairy little mutt." Her eyes narrowed in fury. "He told me he answered an ad for free puppies. O-o-oh! I'm going to. . ." She looked down again at the papers, which were getting carelessly crumpled as her hand tightened into a fist. "Come on, we've got to make a phone call."

She was halfway up the sidewalk before Aaron caught up with her. "Whom are we calling?"

"There's a breeder listed here with a Maitland mailing address. Gregory told me the people who were giving the puppies away were in Maitland."

Fluffy greeted them at the door, obviously delighted by their quick return. "Hello, Judith's Fluffy Heartsong Joy," Judy said, and gave the dog only a cursory pat in passing on her way to the telephone directory. Aaron settled into an armchair and scratched Fluffy behind the ears while Judy found the number and dialed.

Her eyes met his momentarily as she waited for someone to pick up the receiver on the other end of the line. Then she snapped to attention. "Hello. My name is Judy Harte, and I'd like to speak to Gail Grinder about a briard. . . . No, I don't want to buy one now, I wanted to ask about a puppy that you gave away early last month."

A frown of concentration creased her forehead as she listened to the voice on the other end of the line. "I see. Oh, yes, Mrs. Grinder, I'm sure your puppies are of the highest quality. It's just . . . do you happen to recall *selling* one of your puppies to a young man named Gregory Simpson?"

She listened. "Yes. That's right. A female. Um-hum." Judy raised her eyebrows at Aaron, and her words were punctuated by the odd cadence of tethered wrath. "You remember helping him tie a pink satin bow around her neck. . . . *Of course* you were concerned that the ribbon be tied correctly so that it wouldn't tighten and choke the puppy. Mrs. Grinder, I wonder if you could tell me what the purchase price of the puppy was. Yes, he bought her for me, and I was thinking of taking out an insurance policy. I see. Thank you, Mrs. Grinder. That's what I needed to know."

She waited long enough for Mrs. Grinder to hang up and then slammed the phone in place. "That . . . brat! That . . . conniving . . . juvenile delinquent!" she stormed. "Four hundred dollars. Now where in the hell am I supposed to come up with that much money to pay him back?"

Without waiting for a reply, she flopped down on the couch, crossing her arms over her waist. "He must have known I'd find out sooner or later, but he was counting on the fact that once I got attached to Fluffy I'd just laugh it off. Well, he's got another think coming! If I have to pay him back twenty dollars per month . . ."

As if just remembering that she was not the only person in the room, she stopped in midsentence to cast a scowl at Aaron. "What the hell are you laughing at?"

He sobered immediately, or rather tried to with only partial success. "Can't you see the humor in the situation? The kid was trying to do something grand, and he couldn't even *tell* you what he'd done. Imagine how frustrating it must be for him.''

"Why didn't he just answer a 'free puppy' ad? He knew all I wanted was a scruffy little dog.''

"You said it yourself, Judy. He's only nineteen, an overgrown youngster. It probably appealed to his sense of romance to be doing something splendid for you without your even knowing about it.''

Judy sighed. "Maybe I'll see the humor later. Right now I'd just like to pinch his head off, or maybe I could ship him off to reform school. And I *am* going to reimburse him.''

"Why? He wanted to do something grandiose for you. Why not let him have his moment of splendor?''

"*His* moment of splendor? Aaron, Gregory's never worked a day in his life. How do you think his parents would feel about his buying me a champion pooch with the allowance they give him?''

Aaron felt as though a bullet had just gone whizzing past his head. *Gregory's parents. Virginia Simpson. His boss's wife and his mother's sorority sister. God, Judy would hate the whole sordid situation.*

Luckily Judy was too preoccupied with her own reactions to notice Aaron's sudden seriousness, and she continued thinking aloud. "If I thought he was subsisting on peanut-butter sandwiches in order to accomplish this great feat of generosity, I'd be impressed, but he's not. He's a spoiled-rotten kid who squanders money, and I refuse to be a squanderee.''

"A *squanderee*?" Aaron repeated, his humor returning in the form of a chuckle. He moved to the couch and threw his arms around Judy and hugged her spontaneously as though she were a cherished teddy bear, and all thoughts of Virginia Simpson and his devil's deal with her evaporated.

They spread the old blanket Judy kept for picnics on the grassy, sloping bank of the lake, just a few feet from the water. "I was thinking about you at work yesterday," Aaron said when they'd finished their meal and were enjoying the serenity of the setting. "What do schoolteachers do on the day after Thanksgiving when there's no school to teach?"

Laughing, Judy said, "What ninety percent of the female population does the day after Thanksgiving—shop."

"Did you find anything other than sore feet?"

"A few bruised ribs. The malls were pandemonium, and the toy stores were sheer insanity."

"Toy stores?"

"Kevin's not the only little person on my list. There's Ronnie's two kids in Germany and my sister's three in Virginia."

"You have just the one sister?"

"One is enough."

He cocked an eyebrow curiously. "Is that more than the usual sibling rivalry I hear?"

"Not really. It's just..." She frowned slightly. "It wasn't easy being a short, serious genius and having the original dumb blonde for a little sister."

"You were jealous of her?" he asked, surprised.

"Blond hair, blue eyes, tall and willowy, with a bust measurement higher than her IQ? Every female in the school was jealous of Didi Harte. If she hadn't been so *nice*, one of them would have probably scratched her eyes out."

"But you were so bright, Judy."

"Oh, yes. Brilliant. But put us side by side and do you think the guys were impressed by my grasp of the theory of relativity? They could *see* what she had up front. Didi sparkled like gold dust, and I was as exciting as iron ore. My winning the regional number-sense competition certainly couldn't generate as much excitement as her being named head twirler."

She grinned at Aaron. "That sounded adolescent, didn't it? That was years ago."

He soothed her hair, letting his hand linger on her scalp for an instant. "I'm seeing vulnerabilities I would never have imagined you with. I can't imagine a woman like you being insecure."

"I think I always suspected that she was smarter than I was. She always knew exactly how to get what she wanted. Guys stood in line to do her homework for her."

"You wouldn't have wanted anybody doing your homework for you, would you?"

"And ruin my grade point average?" she quipped. "Anyway, that was a long time ago. Didi became a receptionist in an insurance brokerage firm, married her boss and started having babies, which is exactly what she wanted to do, and I quit trying to be an astronaut just because that's what everyone else thought I should be, and now everyone's happy except my father, who thinks I'm hiding my light under a bushel."

"What made you quit?" he asked. "You were so close."

"To a Ph.D.? Do you think that last piece of parchment would have made me happy?"

He shrugged his shoulders. "You must have worked hard to make it even halfway. It seems a shame that you didn't have the satisfaction of getting it."

With a serene smile on her lips, she shook her head, rejecting his reasoning. "That's where you're wrong. I had the satisfaction of *not* getting it, and it felt...I don't know, wonderful. Like watching a pinwheel spin in the breeze."

His eyes swept adoringly over her face. "You and your pinwheels!"

"When I came to stay with Uncle Brad and Aunt Martha, I was devastated over the delay in getting my degree. It took me a while to realize that I had come very close to killing myself trying to get it. But once I accepted the fact that I was going to have to sit out a whole semester, an odd thing happened—I wasn't disappointed anymore, I was just...relieved. I went out and got the first job I'd ever had." She smiled. "At Disney World."

Aaron found that amusing, too, for he grinned back at her.

"I thought they'd put me in some kind of a suit," she continued, "you know, Minnie Mouse or one of the three pigs, but I wound up being a cashier in a gift shop. Talk about work! And during the Christmas tourist rush! It was wild and crazy. But Main Street in the Magic Kingdom is a good place to launch into a childhood."

Her eyes met his. "I never had one, you see. It was a phase of my life I skipped. I never played, I learned. It's hard to be awed by a rainbow when you understand that it's just light passing through droplets of water. Other kids looked at kaleidoscopes and saw a miracle—I saw colored beads and mirrors."

She was suddenly solemn, so serious that Aaron sensed her change of mood and reached out for her hand to let her know that he was there, listening, hearing.

"I didn't have a lot of close friends. We brains weren't 'chums,' we were just people who'd been thrown together by social isolation and fraternized as a result. I sent a Christmas card to a classmate at M.I.T., the closest thing to a 'chum' I'd ever had. She wrote back all the campus news. Bret Winslow had killed himself when his thesis project fell apart, and Cynthia Barron was convalescing in a posh 'rest facility' following a mental collapse.''

She closed her eyes and shuddered at remembered pain, then opened them and looked at Aaron again. ''That's when I knew I wasn't going back. I would have if the degree meant anything to me. But I realized that it didn't. It wasn't important, it was just what was expected of me. All my life I'd been doing what was expected of me. I was tired of it. I was a twenty-four-year-old genius who'd never made an independent decision. I'd been pushed and prodded and accelerated, but I'd never been treated as though I were a human being with emotions as well as intellect.''

Her green eyes were liquid with intensity as they pleaded with his for understanding. ''I had been old for so long, Aaron. I had to be young before it was too late. I was a social infant. So I stayed on Main Street and started looking at life through the eyes of the kids who came in to buy toys. It took over a year for me to gather my fill of the magic I'd missed and face the fact that I couldn't stay on Main Street checking out stuffed Mickey Mice for the rest of my life.''

''So you wound up teaching middle school.''

''I didn't wind up teaching, Aaron. It wasn't something I settled for. I *decided* to teach because it's what I wanted to do, and I went back to school part-time until I finished the courses I needed for my certificate. And I chose the level I wanted to teach.''

''So you could get them before they'd had the curiosity bred out of them.''

She grinned sheepishly. ''Have I been on this soapbox before?''

''I could look at you and listen to you all day when your eyes are flashing like that. You're the most tenacious person I've ever met." Reading her mixed reaction to the comment, he tweaked her nose with his forefinger. "That, lady, was a compliment, so you can draw those claws back in."

"Do I seem defensive?" she said. "It's just that I've found myself defending what I do ever since I decided to do it. I was at the point where if one more person said, 'Honey, you could do anything in the world you want to do. Research. Private industry. Why would you throw it away in a public middle school? At least go to the college level,' I would have punched them out."

"'Why *did* you decide on middle school?' I ask gingerly," he said.

She shrugged. "Who knows? I got used to being around kids? I wanted *someone* to be teaching science the way it ought to be taught? Why would I care why it's what I'm happy doing, so long as I get to keep on doing it?"

Aaron's eyes narrowed appraisingly. "I'll bet you're damned good at it, too."

"You're damned right I am."

"That explains a few mysteries—such as why you came at me with your fangs showing the first time we met. It wasn't fair of you to assume I wouldn't respect what you do just because I go to work in a suit."

"That assumption was founded on past experience."

"Not on any experiences with me, it wasn't."

"Do you want an apology?" she said, cocking her head playfully.

"An apology?" he said. His mood had changed, too, but not to playfulness. She felt the sensual heat emanating from him as his eyes burned into her. "I don't want an apology, I want atonement." His grin was positively wicked. "I'll exact it the next time we're alone."

Judy felt the flush rising in her face. It didn't take her genius to hear the innuendo in his voice. So this is what it was like to engage in erotic banter. Not crude sex talk, but the subtle teasing of the senses. Thrilling was the word that best described it. She was tingling all over, even inside. Especially inside. "May I ask you a question?"

"Shoot," he said gamely.

Without warning, she leaned forward and nipped his shoulder with her teeth. Aaron reflexively jerked away from the assault, and a pout formed on her lips. "It works in all the books," she said.

"What are you up to, you little monkey?"

"The question was supposed to be 'Does this turn you on?' Everybody bites shoulders in books, and it drives men crazy. Obviously we're dealing with real life here."

Aaron threw back his head and laughed uproariously. Then, still chuckling, he reached out and gathered her into his arms. "You are so dear, sweet Judy. Believe me, you can bite my shoulder, and I promise to go crazy... *when* the time and circumstances are right."

She pulled away from him and sniffed petulantly. He picked up a strand of her hair and rubbed it between his fingers. "It'll be different when we're alone and..."

"And?" she challenged.

"It would help if I weren't wearing a shirt." Making a show of rubbing his wound, he added, "And you could be a little gentler—maybe nibble a little instead of chomping."

"I'll make a note of that."

Unconsciously she had twisted away from him, turning her back to him. He reached up and kneaded her shoulders, letting his thumbs trace tantalizing circles on her neck. Then he whispered in her ear, "You don't have to try so hard, Judy. I'm not going to be disappointed."

Judy felt a poignant and totally irrational need to cry, but held back. How could he be so sensitive to what she was thinking and feeling? It made her wonder if he knew how badly she needed to hear him say he loved her—and if he was refraining from saying it because he didn't want to be less than sincere.

She sighed, letting the tension in her muscles succumb to the relaxing motion of his hands. J. Hollis Aaron was nothing if not sincere.

They had time to go through the science museum before the planetarium show started. Judy played guide, taking him first to the huge pendulum and pointing out the cardboard boxes it knocked over as the earth rotated them into its path. "Mind-boggling, isn't it, the way we think of the earth as stable. The concept of terra firma. But it's constantly moving beneath our feet."

Aaron's arm was across her back, and he tightened his hold on her. "I've had the sensation of the earth's moving under my feet ever since I met you."

"Flatterer," she said. *Flattery's going to get him everything, and he knows it. Oh, Aaron, will I ever make you love me?*

They walked to the pinboard, where stickpins were suspended from the holes of a fine wire mesh and it was possible to create elusive images in the silver surface of the heads of the pins by pushing up on the pins from below. Aaron wrote a message, letter by letter: "U- R- C-U-T-E." "Your turn," he said.

She was tempted to write "I", draw a heart and then spell his name. Why not tell him how she felt? she wondered. The answer was quick in coming. Her common sense was uncommonly, irritatingly talkative today. *Because you don't know how he feels. Because you don't want to pressure him. Because you're a coward.* She wrote "U- R- 2."

"Isn't it a stroke of fortune, two adorable people like us finding each other?" Aaron said.

"Watch out, world," she agreed, and with their arms entwined they entered the main room of the museum. "My students get extra credit for coming here. This is the best of hands-on science, and it's on their level. And this—" she stopped in front of a display of wind-powered generators "—is my favorite exhibit."

"Variations on the pinwheel theme," Aaron said. "What is it with you and pinwheels, anyway?"

"Have you ever noticed the way a child's face lights up when he's watching a pinwheel?"

"No. To be honest, I haven't been around kids much."

"It's magic," she said. "I used to look at pinwheels and see wind pushing against a resistant surface. If you take the time to watch enough children look at a pinwheel, eventually you see magic. I don't ever want to lose that magic, Aaron. I don't want to let go of it. It's too precious."

Aaron touched her cheek with his forefinger. The simple gesture, coupled with his almost unbearably sweet smile, held the intimate overtones of an erotic promise. Judy hardly heard his softly spoken words through the pulse throbbing in her ears: "I can see the magic in your eyes, Judy."

An enchantment tiptoed over Judy's senses in feather-soled shoes, tickling and titillating. A timeless communication had passed between them as their eyes met, too basic and fundamental for words. The words had not been "I love you," but the feeling was unmistakable, and for a brief moment suspended in time she was aware only of Aaron and the spell that spun around them like a gossamer web.

Aaron was caught up in it, too, this spinning vortex of emotion the poets called falling in love. The thought that he should be surprised flitted through his mind and was dismissed. There was no room for surprise when he was filled so completely with the wonder of what had happened, what he'd never believed could happen, what had always seemed to him to be the whimsy of emotional fools.

Quite simply, he wanted Judy Harte in every tender way it was possible to want a woman, and *needed* her in every way a man could need a woman. He needed her smiles and the look in her eyes that told him he was the most special man in the world to her. He needed the scent of her perfume and the warmth of her body next to his. He needed the insight of her steel-trap mind and the frivolousness of the pinwheels she collected and the gentleness of her nature.

He wasn't ready to think about where his feelings would lead. They were too new, too intense. But he had moved beyond denial into the realm of acknowledgment, and he found himself peculiarly at ease with emotions previously alien to him. He grasped the significance of the moment if not the ramifications of it. This was the moment that sliced his life into two segments. For the rest of his life, he would separate time in his mind—everything would be either before or after he fell in love with Judy Harte.

Two boisterous eight-year-olds had approached the exhibit, and in their fight to see who worked the blowers that set the windmills and turbines into action first, one of the boys stumbled into Judy and Aaron. The child stared at them in wide-eyed surprise. Then, remembering his manners, he mumbled, "Excuse me," before turning back to the exhibit.

The interruption forced them back to the reality that they were in a public place, but the magic remained with them as they strolled from exhibit to exhibit holding hands. Eventually they reached the base of a small bank of stairs that led to the top of a wooden platform. Mounted on the wall above the platform was a concave dish that resembled a miniature satellite dish. It faced an identical disk mounted on the opposite wall above a similar platform. "What do you do here?" Aaron asked.

"You whisper across the room," Judy said. Tilting her head toward the platform, she added, "Go on up. I'll go to the other side."

"What do I do?"

"Just listen, and when I talk to you, talk back." Across the room, she whispered into the disk. "Can you hear me?"

"Yes," came the reply, "now what?"

"Say something."

"What?"

She cast him one of her most menacing frustrated-teacher looks, turned back to the disk and said, "Mother Goose rhymes. Naughty limericks. Shakespeare. Whatever pops into your mind."

"I think I love you."

Judy froze, afraid if she moved the words he'd spoken would somehow dissipate into nonexistence. "Judy?" he said after a very long time. Very slowly she turned so she could see him, and their eyes made contact across the empty space between them. It occurred to her that she should say the same thing back to him, give voice to the thrilling emotion that filled her to overflowing, but she just stood there, mute, staring at him, thinking how ridiculously handsome he was and how phenomenally lucky she was to have such a ridiculously handsome man tell her he loved her. And his smile! How could she ever have thought of him as a Treadmill Clone when he had a smile like that. She basked in the warmth of it from across the room.

Gradually it grew a bit mischievous, taking on the naughty lilt of a grin. He turned to speak into the disk, and she knew what he said would be witty and amusing.

"I crave your body, too."

The sound of her delighted laughter echoed through the air and reverberated in the disk in front of him. He could hear the music in her voice when she said, "Most men just like me for my brain."

"Today's first showing of the planetarium production *Starship Voyage* will begin in ten minutes," a voice announced pre-emptively through a speaker. "Those wishing to view this production should proceed to the planetarium entrance, where the doors will open in five minutes."

"Guess that's our cue," Judy said into the disk. "Meet you in the center of the room."

They sat in the back row of seats while the last-minute stragglers milled about searching for the scattered empty places. Aaron picked up Judy's hand and held it loosely in his own, rubbing his thumb over the softness of her skin.

"Did you mean it?" she asked.

He didn't answer her immediately, but his hand tightened around hers, trapping it firmly as though he was afraid she might try to pull it away. She heard him inhale sharply, then exhale slowly. "I meant it." The lights began to dim, but not so quickly that she didn't see the smile playing at his lips. "All of it," he said. Soon they were in absolute darkness, the only sound in the room the shuffling of restless children. Judy gasped as something touched her hair and then realized that it was Aaron, brushing it back and away from her face. A shiver of pure stimulation racked the entire length of her body as he caught the lobe of her ear in his teeth and tugged gently on the gold stud earrings she was wearing. His tongue flitted over the top rim of her ear, and his single whispered word puffed into her ear like a tiny cloud of titillation. "Later."

She turned to say something, but he shushed her by placing a forefinger over her lips. "The show's starting."

A sound track surrounded them with the night sounds of crickets and hoot owls, and overhead a miniaturized universe sprang to life through the wonders of electronics. Judy threaded her fingers through Aaron's and whispered, "You're so good at this, Aaron, and I . . ."

"You're a bright girl, Judy. You'll learn."

Hours later, as they sat arm to arm on a banquette behind a tiny table in an Italian restaurant, nibbling on breadsticks between minestrone and linguine, Judy risked stroking the top of his thigh gently with her fingertips, watching his face, fascinated, as she did so. His eyes narrowed as he looked at her, and his voice was huskier than usual. "You're about an inch away from indecency, young lady."

She smiled smugly as her fingers tightened around a sinew of well-developed thigh muscle and his eyes widened in surprise. "And you're about an inch away from insanity."

He uttered a sound that was half growl, half groan, then regarded her through narrowed eyelids. "Perceptive little monkey, aren't you?"

"I know the fringes of insanity when I see it," she parried.

"Especially when you precipitate it."

"Are you insinuating that I'm driving you crazy?"

"I never insinuate the obvious."

The waitress served their entrées. "I understand they're working on nutritional therapy to cure some types of insanity," Judy said, plunging her fork into the pasta.

"The deprivation making me crazy isn't nutritional," Aaron said.

"You could try substitution," she suggested.

"I'd be a fat man within a week," was his wry reply.

They took Fluffy for a lazy lap around the lake after returning to the condo. When they reached Judy's door again, Aaron leaned his elbow against the jamb and said, "I'd like to come in—just for a few minutes. Just long enough to tell you good-night."

Judy nodded and opened the door. Inside, she bent to unclip the leash from Fluffy's collar and then stood up. Alone finally, mere inches apart, she and Aaron were suddenly self-conscious in each other's presence. "It was a wonderful day," she said. "Thank you for everything."

"Thank *you*," he said. "I would never have thought of the planetarium."

"Aaron—"

"Judy—"

And then they were in each other's arms, their mouths fused in a deep, searing kiss, their bodies touching full length. Judy massaged the hard muscles that crisscrossed his shoulders, then threaded her fingers through his hair.

Aaron cupped the roundness of her hips in his hands and pressed his thighs against hers. His mouth left hers to press urgent kisses on her cheek, behind her ear, on her neck. "You're so strong in my blood that I feel I could assimilate you," he said, "just absorb you so that you're part of me."

"I feel the same way," she said, clinging to him, holding on to him for support as the sensations he stoked in her spread through her limbs with an enervating effect.

For several minutes he just held her, stroking her hair, raining tiny kisses on the top of her head while she listened to the comforting rhythm of his heart under her ear.

"You know that you're special, don't you?" he asked abruptly. "It's not just this; it's much more than this." He felt the motion of her cheek against his shoulder as she nodded, and cupped her chin with his fingertips, raising her head so that their eyes met. "It's time, Judy. Let's go out tomorrow night—get all dressed up and go someplace with candlelight and soft music."

She nodded somberly, her eyes large and limpid and filled with the light of love.

"You know what I'm asking," he said, and she nodded again.

"One of us has to do some shopping."

"I will," she said.

He hugged her one last time before letting her go, and was halfway through the door before he reached out and touched his fingertips lingeringly to her cheek and said, "I love you."

Several minutes went by before Judy realized she'd let him leave without telling him that she loved him, too.

Chapter Ten

Didn't wake you up, did I? It's almost noon." The contagious cheer in Jack Sawyer's voice carried electronically through the phone wires.

"No," Aaron assured his fellow Butterfield Investments vice president. "I've been up and about for hours."

"I was thinking of doing some shopping this afternoon after the meeting at Simpson's house. Thought you might want to ride together and stop at the mall on the way home. I despise shopping alone, and I can't shop for Beth's gift with Beth along."

"Sure," Aaron said. "There's a couple of things I need to shop for, too. But I can't stay late. I need to be home by six or so."

"That ought to give us an hour and a half. That's more time than any man should voluntarily spend in a crowded shopping mall. I'll pick you up about one-thirty."

* * *

Later, when Aaron got in the car, Jack said, "This is your first 'Last Sunday' meeting, isn't it?" Aaron nodded. "Theoretically they're a good idea. We get a lot of the end-of-the-month stuff covered so that we're not so pressed during the rush at the office. But you'd think Daddy Simpson would have given us a break on the Sunday after Thanksgiving. It's bad enough we had to work Friday while he was vacationing in the Poconos. I don't think they were flying back until this morning. I'll bet Virginia's thrilled with fixing high tea for the troops an hour after she gets off the plane."

Ah, yes. Virginia Simpson. Aaron couldn't suppress a small smile as he thought of the story he had to share with Virginia. Surely even she would see the humor in Gregory's having bought his "older woman" a pedigreed show dog that he'd passed off as a mutt. She should be relieved to know exactly where the money had gone.

"Do you have any idea what you're going to buy Beth?" Aaron asked to hold up his end of the conversation.

"She wants a watch, one of those with the big, bright faces and no numbers. And I usually buy her a bottle of her favorite perfume. A bottle lasts almost exactly a year, so it's become a tradition. What about you?" Jack asked. "Anything in particular you're looking for?"

"I'll probably sniff around the perfume counter while we're there."

Jack chanced a glance away from traffic to raise his eyebrows at Aaron. "This wouldn't have anything to do with your 'better offer' on Thanksgiving, would it?"

Aaron smiled guiltily and shrugged his shoulders. Jack laughed as he turned his attention back to the road. "You don't let any grass grow under your feet, do you, Aaron?"

Not where Judy's concerned, thought Aaron, as a fresh wave of longing for the evening ahead surged through him. He hadn't expected to be able to sleep the night before, but he'd fallen asleep easily and awakened refreshed, brimming with a euphoric sense of optimism and well-being. He couldn't remember having felt this way since childhood, so confident that everything in the world was right and beautiful. Memories of the day before filled him with happiness, and thoughts of the evening ahead filled him with sweet anticipation. He felt he could sing or dance or simply frolic through a meadow and all his music and motion would hold an ethereal beauty—this from a grown man who couldn't carry a tune in a bucket!

Bob Borden was standing on the doorstep when they approached Simpson's door, and almost immediately Trace Simpson opened the door. "My goodness, I wasn't expecting all three of you at once. Come in, come in."

The standard small talk was exchanged. The three vice presidents assured Simpson they'd had more than their share of turkey on Thanksgiving, and Simpson assured them there was more-than-adequate snow in the Poconos. Virginia Simpson came in to say hello and offered the men soft drinks, wine coolers and coffee, which she served after they had settled around the massive maple dining table with their portfolios open.

They were deep in discussion of the success of a particular investment package when Gregory walked in the front door wearing chic tennis shorts and carrying a leather-sheathed tennis racquet. Spying the meeting in progress, he nodded sheepishly and would have disappeared into the back rooms of the house if his father hadn't stopped him. "Come on in and give us a proper hello son. Gentlemen, you remember my son, Gregory." Then, as an afterthought, he said, "You may not have met Gregory yet,

Aaron. Gregory, this is our new vice president of investments, J. Hollis Aaron."

Gregory's head actually snapped when he recognized
Aaron. "J. Hollis?"

Aaron smiled charmingly, as though delightfully surprised, hoping no one else recognized the less-than-
enthusiastic quality of Gregory Simpson's attitude toward him. "Hello, Gregory," he said evenly. "I didn't put
the two Simpsons together." To Trace he said, "Gregory
and I are neighbors."

"I guess you are," Trace Simpson said, as though the
possibility had just occurred to him. "You did take a lease-
purchase option on one of our condos, didn't you? I
should have had Gregory look you up and introduce himself."

Gregory excused himself as soon as politely possible,
and Trace put the the business meeting back on track with
an incisive question regarding a new construction project
they were considering adding to a package being assem-
bled. They had finished their general business and Trace
and Jack were hashing over an accounting problem when
Virginia returned an hour later and offered to refill cups.
Sensing the end of the meeting, everyone declined, and she
began gathering the empty cups.

"I'll help you, Mrs. Simpson," Aaron volunteered, and
followed her to the kitchen with a cup and saucer in each
hand.

"In all the years Trace has been hosting these little Sun-
day-afternoon soirees, you're the first vice president who's
ever volunteered to help clear the table," Virginia said.

"Actually, I had an ulterior motive," Aaron told her. "I
thought you might like to know how your son has been
spending your money."

Virginia put the dishes she was holding in the sink and turned to face him. "You found out?"

"Yes. Quite by accident." Quickly he told her about the letter from the A.K.C. and Judy's surprise at learning she owned the son of a champion.

"Kids!" Virginia said, rolling her eyes. "You'd think I'd have learned with the first three."

"Judy's going to give him what-for when she sees him again," Aaron said. "Believe me, he'll be properly chastened. She's a schoolteacher, you know. If I were you I wouldn't say a word to him."

"It'll surface sooner or later," Virginia said. "I think I'll just let things simmer along naturally." She took the dishes from his hands and impulsively stood on tiptoe to kiss his cheek. "Thank you, Aaron. I know you were uncomfortable about this whole thing, and I do appreciate your help in this matter."

"They'll wonder what's taking me so long."

Virginia nodded. "You'd better be getting back."

He was barely out of sight when she heard a movement from the opposite side of the room. She looked up to see Gregory framed by the door that led from the breakfast nook to the screened Florida room.

"What matter, Mother?" he asked.

"Gregory..." she said.

"I want to know all about it," he said.

"It's nothing you should be concerned with."

"It obviously concerns me," he said petulantly. "Are you going to tell me, or do I call Daddy and Mr. Aaron in here so we can all discuss it."

Virginia felt ill. Sometimes it was difficult to like the person her son had become, even though she loved him. The stinker was blackmailing her, and she no choice but to tell him what he wanted to know. Trace would never understand how she could spy on their son or place his employee in such an embarrassing and compromising situation. Lord, she'd never hear the end of it if Trace got involved.

Reluctantly she followed Gregory into the Florida room and sank defeatedly into the rattan chair. "I want to know everything," Gregory said. "Everything."

She frowned at him. "There are times when I wish you were five years old again," she said. She'd give his backside a good tanning if he were.

"The problem is," he said, "you still *treat* me like I'm five years old."

The sounds of car doors slamming and engines starting carried from the driveway out front, and from inside the sound of cheering football fans on the television carried to the porch. *Oh, Lord,* thought Virginia, *I didn't have a chance to warn Aaron. If he's really interested in this Harte girl, all this could backfire in his face.*

Aaron selected a cameo brooch for his mother, who was fond of cameos, while Jack fretted over which watch to buy his wife. Then, after they'd wandered to the cosmetics department, he asked directions to the counter that sold Allure. There he picked out the deluxe gift set with cologne, perfume, body lotion, body powder and matching porcelain powder shaker and atomizer. This he had giftwrapped in gold foil with a red bow for Christmas. He also bought an Allure-scented candle in a porcelain holder and had it wrapped in a pretty pastel paisley paper. He would give it to Judy tonight and ask her to light it and put it on the bedside table.

Hours later, as he approached Judy's condo with the paisley package in his hand, Aaron was charged with anticipation . . . of her beauty, of the feel of her body against his as he embraced her, of the sweetness of kissing her. She would be all dressed up, and her cheeks would be slightly flushed with her own anticipation, and her smile—that phenomenal Judy Harte smile—would flash a welcome in her lovely green eyes.

Fluffy responded instantly to the chime of the doorbell, barking hysterically, but it seemed to Aaron that Judy was taking longer than usual to answer the door.

A person would think you're anxious, he thought wryly, and shifted his weight from one foot to the other.

The moment the door opened it was obvious that something was horribly amiss. Instead of greeting him, Judy simply left the door gaping and walked toward the living room, leaving Aaron to wrestle Fluffy out of the notion of bolting outside.

She was wearing a pair of faded jeans that were frayed at the hem and the Teachers Are a Class Act T-shirt she'd had on the first time he'd seen her. Her hair hung in unencumbered disarray. Ordinarily Aaron would have found her careless dishabille charming, but the sense of foreboding prickling his scalp didn't allow him the luxury of admiring her casual charm. After wrestling Fluffy inside and securing the door, he hurried after Judy in time to see her flop unceremoniously onto the couch, hug her knees to her chest and prop her forehead on her knees.

"Judy?" he asked.

Very slowly she raised her head to direct wide accusing eyes at him. Her silence was more ominous than a shrieked accusation.

"What's wrong, Judy?"

She stared, unseeing, at the pinwheels next to the wall. "Gregory was waiting for me when I got home from the drugstore."

Aaron sank onto the couch next to her, eyeing the box in his hands, its bright wrappings and pert bow now so obscenely out of place. With a sniff of disgust, he set it on the coffee table. Its pastel frivolity mocked him as he turned back to Judy. "How much did he tell you?"

The sob that had been barely contained behind Judy's mask of stoicism burst from her throat. "Oh, God, Aaron, how could you?" She buried her face in her hands.

"It's not what you think," he said. "It's not as bad as it seems."

Her head snapped up. The wet stain of tears streaked her cheeks. A hard knot of tension formed in Aaron's guts. How could he have hurt her this way? He'd never wanted to hurt her.

"It's bad, Aaron," she said. "And so very, very ugly."

He touched her arm with no thought beyond comforting her, but she jerked it away from him and shouted, "No!"

"Judy, I know Gregory probably put an ugly inflection on the situation."

She hugged her knees tighter and rocked back and forth and swallowed a sob, trying to gather her voice. Aaron thought he'd die from the pain she was feeling, the pain he'd caused her.

"You're so eloquent," she said bitterly, staring at the pinwheels again. "'An ugly inflection.'" Finally she faced him, her beautiful face contorted with misery. "He didn't have to put an ugly inflection on it, Aaron. It was ugly enough. You tried to play God in our lives. How could you do that? How could you and Gregory's mother make judgments about my character and decide to manipulate me?"

"That's not the way it was, Judy. She was concerned."

"*She* had a right to be. Right or wrong, at least she had a legitimate interest in Gregory's welfare. What's your excuse?"

"She was my boss's wife, Judy. What she was asking didn't seem—"

"Seduce a stranger away from her son? Assume she's a fortune hunter and outwit her at her own game? Treat a perfect stranger like...an object instead of a human being with thoughts and feelings...spy on her." She buried her face again and wept.

Aaron instinctively reached out to comfort her, but she shrank from him again. "Don't touch me!" she shrieked. "I can't think straight when you touch me." She took a deep breath, then exhaled in a ragged shudder as she wiped her cheeks with the back of her hand. "Mrs. Simpson certainly sent the right man, didn't she? So damned virile and charming. Oh, I saw it at first. All the ambition and the anything-for-success personality. But the charm blinded me."

A pitiful wail rose from her throat. "You just couldn't do anything halfway, could you? You must have known right away that I wasn't interested in Gregory, but you couldn't stop in the middle of a job."

"It wasn't that way, Judy. Not after I got to know you."

"What else would you do for your boss's wife? How far would you go?"

"Judy—"

"Dammit!" she shouted. Then she whispered, "And damn you." A shudder passed through her body. "Why couldn't you just leave me alone?" She haphazardly wiped the tears from her cheeks again. "Damn you, why did you have to make me fall in love with you?"

"Because I fell in love with you," he said. "I didn't romance you to lure you away from Gregory. I wasn't 'giving my all' for Virginia Simpson. I met you, I wanted you, and I fell in love with you.'' He repeated the phrase emphatically. ''I love you.''

Her eyes snapped with anger. ''You wouldn't know the meaning of love if you looked it up in the dictionary. Do you love me the way you loved Melissa? Or your two other ex-fiancées? How many women have you said that to, Aaron?''

''Virginia Simpson certainly got talkative, didn't she?'' he said, wanting to grab Judy and shake her, make her understand that what he felt for her was different and special. But she wouldn't believe him, wouldn't let herself believe him, and who could blame her?

Inside his chest, his heart felt as though it was being ripped into ragged strips. She was hurt, as she damned well had a right to be. He would have cut off his hand at the wrist if it would have taken away her pain, but nothing could work that miracle. He could set himself afire to demonstrate his remorse and she'd still be sitting there, hurting with his treachery. God, how had he managed to sully anything as special as his love for Judy? Surely he was the only man in the world who could debase something as pure as that.

''Your love is meaningless,'' she said, sniffing. ''It's empty, like a promise you don't plan to keep. Like those commitments you make and don't follow through on.''

He tried once more to pull her into his arms. ''You're hurt, Judy, but we can work through the hurt.''

She hadn't jerked away from him, but she didn't yield, either, didn't soften under his touch. It was more as if she was beyond caring and her resistance was exhausted.

Her voice had a weak, faraway quality. ''This isn't a scratch, Aaron. We can't put a Band-Aid on it and wait for it to go away. It's a gaping wound. When it heals . . . Oh,

God, I don't know if it'll ever heal." She reached to cover her face with her hands, and he pressed his advantage and tried to guide her head to his shoulder. Her strength returned from some inner source. "No!" she said, and pushed his arms away. "I want you to leave."

"Judy—"

"I mean it, Aaron. I want you to go. Now."

"I can't just walk off and leave you." *Could he?*

Her silence was deafening as her eyes bored into him, accusing, offering no forgiveness, no understanding. Perhaps, he thought, she had none to give. Maybe the pain was so great, had filled her so full, that there was no room left for anything else.

"It's insane, Judy."

"It's not as insane as my letting you stay here and make an even bigger fool of me."

Aaron nodded and swallowed a sob, mortified that he was close to crying. His mind was adjusting to the fact that he had no choice, that the love he felt for her in every inch of his body and every breath he drew wasn't going to salvage the situation immediately and might never be enough to salvage it.

He walked to the door with a sluggish gait, as though he were wearing heavy weights on his ankles. Fluffy trailed after him, her tail curled in hope of a romp outside. Aaron paused with his hand on the doorknob, choked back the persistent lump in his throat and said hoarsely, "I've got to tell you one more time, Judy: I love you. I know it seems meaningless now, but maybe later, when you think about it . . ." He couldn't go on. It was taking all his strength to walk away from her, not knowing if he'd ever see her smile again.

Or if he would ever smile again himself.

* * *

He'd imagined what it would be like when he saw her again, but he was still unprepared for the pain that knifed through him at the sight of her. She was standing in the pool at the spa, talking to several women as they waited for the water-aerobics class to begin. He took advantage of the fact that her back was to the large hall window to drink in the sight of her, petite, perfect and exquisitely feminine.

The water-aerobics instructor, tall and sleek in a black tank suit, brushed past him on her way from the dressing room to the pool. Music from the soft-rock sound track the challenge-workout instructor used for warm-ups floated up the hallway. Aaron took a half step away from the window, thinking that if he didn't hurry he'd miss the class. Then he stopped, not giving a damn if he missed it. What was a workout when he could look at Judy?

The instructor had taken her shower and was stepping into the pool, calling the class to order. En masse, the participants began jogging the length of the pool.

What the hell! thought Aaron. After a mad dash under the shower, he leaped in the pool and made it to the middle in time to join the joggers on their return lap from the far end. It didn't take him long to maneuver his way toward Judy. After shock, the expression that claimed her eyes was one of pure venom. "Didn't you miss a turn somewhere? The *challenge* workout is down the hall."

He found her hostility strangely comforting. Certainly being a target for her verbal barbs was preferable to being ignored. "This class was recommended by a friend. She says it's fun."

"Everyone, chin to the chest now," the instructor said. "Now to the left shoulder. Look left. And look right."

"Look beyond the nose on your face and you'll see that I love you," Aaron said. Judy turned her back to him.

"Now reach those arms out. Left. Right. Stretch. Very good."

"The first fiancée was my high-school sweetheart," Aaron said, stepping close behind her so that only Judy could hear. "She was the first girl I ever made love to. We were eighteen when I gave her a promise ring. Her father sent her to France for a summer study program to cool things off between us."

"I wish my father would send *me* to France," Judy said.

The instructor said, "Okay, time for shoulder, shoulder, shoulder out. Right hand first. Let's go."

"She fell for a starving artist."

"I'd take a starving artist over an unscrupulous clod any day."

"Okay, folks, let's twist. Twist left and then right. Look behind you when you twist."

Aaron made a silly face and waved when Judy looked in his direction. She frowned and ignored him the next time around.

"My second engagement was during my senior year in college. We actually got as far as a ring with a diamond in it. We'd been dating several months and all her sorority sisters were getting engaged, and it seemed like the thing to do at the time."

"Did you use that line when you slipped the ring on her finger?" Judy snapped.

"She was more excited about blowing out the candle at her sorority candlelight ceremony than about being engaged."

"Okay, let's rotate those right legs from the knee down. Big circles under the water."

"Anyway, she went to work and I went to grad school, and she was offered a promotion to move to Chicago. I said I wouldn't care much for living in Chicago, and she said I was a male chauvinist who was trying to undermine her career. I asked why she couldn't be successful in Boston or New York, but she went on to Chicago and I stayed at Yale until I graduated and moved on to Wall Street.''

"Switch direction, folks. Circle the other way, same leg.''

"Look,'' Judy said, planting her hands on her waist. "To quote a popular bumper sticker, you must have mistaken me for someone who cares. I find these tales of your past love lives less than scintillating. In fact, I find them repugnant. Now would you mind leaving me alone?''

"Okay, point those toes, then flex that foot. Flex, point, flex, point...''

"Yes, I mind leaving you alone. I love you. And it's not a schoolboy crush or peer pressure this time. I'm a big boy now. I know what I want.''

"The left leg now, folks. Big circles from the knee down.''

"Just like you knew what you wanted with Melissa.''

The barb hit home. Aaron flinched. "Melissa knew what she wanted with me,'' he said. "One day I came home from work and she said, 'It's stupid to maintain two residences. I did your laundry today. It's time you made an honest woman of me.' ''

"Too bad the two of you didn't make it,'' Judy said, switching to the opposite leg in response to the instructor's directions. "Melissa sounds almost as romantic as you are.''

"I don't want to talk—'' Aaron said, and realized he had raised his voice to a level that was drawing the attention of the other people in the class. He began again in a near whisper, "I don't want to talk about Melissa, dammit, I want to talk about us.''

Judy dropped her foot to the bottom of the pool and frowned at him. "What was that wonderful phrase you used about the refrigerator? Oh, yes. 'Frankly, my dear, I don't give a damn!' It's a bit overused, but in this situation it's very apropos. I don't want to talk about us, Aaron. I don't want to talk about your ludicrous track record in love. I don't want to talk to you at all. Now leave me alone!"

This last was said so emphatically that several heads, including that of the instructor, turned to see what was going on. "All right," said the instructor. "Line up on the sides of the pool. We've got a large group today, so we're going to work in two shifts, side to side."

Judy scurried away from Aaron and scowled at him, daring him to come near her. He walked to the opposite side of the pool and faced her.

"All right," the instructor said when everyone was situated. "We're going to start with this side." She pointed to the side Aaron was on. "I want you guys to bunny-hop across the pool. If you don't know the person opposite you, introduce yourself when you get to the other side before you skip back. That's step hop, step hop back."

Judy looked as though she might duck under the water as he advanced toward her. He wouldn't put drowning herself to avoid him past her. Unconsciously he hurried so that he was standing in front of her before she had a chance to take the plunge. He smiled. "Hello. My name is J. Hollis Aaron. The *J* is short for Jerome, and you can call me Jerry if you like, although no one's called me that since junior high, besides my parents."

He saw the moistness in her eyes, the quiver in her chin. *Dammit,* he thought, *why do you have to fight it? Don't you feel what's between us? If you didn't, you wouldn't be crying.*

"Skip back," prompted the instructor. "Step hop, step hop."

Reluctantly Aaron turned, breaking eye contact with her, and tried to remember how to skip. When he reached the pool wall and turned, Judy was gone. Scanning the room in a panic, he caught sight of her just as she passed through the door to the hallway and then watched as she ducked into the women's locker room.

"Hi," said a woman, plump, gray-haired and quite jolly. "My name is Hazel."

"Aaron," he replied, forcing a friendly smile. "It's nice to meet you, Hazel."

Hazel turned and skipped off, and Aaron's gaze drifted back to the locker-room door that barred him from the woman he loved.

We're even now, Judy Harte, he thought morosely. *You said I made a fool of you; now I've made a fool of myself for you.*

"Time for flutter-kicking," the instructor announced cheerfully.

In the shower stall in the ladies' locker room, Judy stood under the spray of warm water and, with her face buried in her hands, bawled like a baby over the unfairness of life. And love. Why did he have to be so wrong for her? *And why couldn't she stop loving him?*

Aaron toweled off as best as he could, and with his clothes still wet from the pool tried in vain to work the edge off his frustration in the weight room. It didn't help. Nothing did. He gave up and headed home.

The first thing he saw when he entered his condo was the perfume he'd bought for her. The pretty gold foil package with the bright red bow that she'd never see, never open. The perfume she'd never wear for him.

In an impulsive assault on the frustration that was eating him up inside, he picked up the package and flung it at the brick fireplace with all his strength. It landed with a heavy thud, a dull noise that provided no satisfaction at all. A wet stain appeared on the foil, dulling it, and grew. The scent of Allure—Judy's scent—penetrated the room, a vaporous fog that taunted him, haunted him. He wanted to wring his hands through his hair and bellow like a man possessed because that was what he was—a man possessed by memories and yearnings and dreams that would never come true.

The next afternoon a potted poinsettia was delivered to Judy's door with a note. When she read the simple, unsigned message, "I won't embarrass you anymore," she carefully put the small florist's card back in its envelope.

Judy felt as if something or someone had died. Late that night, she skulked to the door of his condo and set the paisley package, still unopened, on his doormat. It was like putting flowers on a grave.

Chapter Eleven

A bitter cold descended with the sunset, and Aaron hurried to the house, glad he'd taken the time that morning to shovel the new snow from the flagstone path in the back as well as from the front walk.

"Is that you, Jerry?" his mother called from upstairs.

"Yes, Mom."

Maxine Aaron appeared at the top of the stairs. "I thought maybe your father was home at a reasonable hour for once. You'd think he'd make the effort with his only son visiting."

"It's ski season, Mother. There's fresh snow..."

"And broken bones to mend," she said, finishing the family joke. "I'll be down in a few minutes to keep you company."

Aaron added a log to the fire in the den and stirred the glowing ashes under the grate to make the flame catch quicker. The setters, worn out from loping through snow up to their bellies, settled contentedly on the floor near the fire. Aaron pulled off his boots and set them on the hearth and reverted to his childhood custom of sitting cross-legged on the sofa facing the fire with a wool afghan folded around his shoulders.

When he was a boy, he'd imagined himself an Indian chief sitting in a tepee, wearing the sacred tribal blanket. But there was no room for childhood fantasies in his mind now. It was Judy Harte he was thinking of. She should be here with him, sitting in front of him so he could wrap the blanket around her, too, and they could cuddle in its shared warmth.

His yearning was more than sexual—as much as he would enjoy the feel of her body in his arms, he also needed the cheer of her smile, the lively repartee they shared. He wanted her, all of her, in his life. Forever.

And ever and ever, he thought with a stab of self-pity. The times they'd spent together, the many facets of Judy Harte played repeatedly through his mind—prickliness at being lectured on how she should train her dog; fury at Gregory over the fast one he'd pulled about Fluffy; tenderness as she held her baby cousin; pliancy as she melted in his arms; seriousness when she confessed her sexual inexperience. Her innocence had been an aphrodisiac in itself, and she had been too guileless to realize it. The remembered image of her face after she'd taken a bite of his shoulder, and the way she said, "The question was supposed to be, 'Does this turn you on?'" sent a fresh wave of sadness rolling through him. She hadn't understood the strength of the power she held over him. Even now, just thinking of her, he desired her.

At first he'd been glad for her sake that they hadn't made love. She despised him enough for his duplicity; she would have hated herself for her own culpability if they'd taken that major step. But in the weeks they'd been apart, he'd reconsidered. If they'd made love, maybe the extra bond between them would have been strong enough to overpower her disillusionment. Maybe if they'd made that commitment, shared that ultimate intimacy, they'd be together instead of apart. If she'd had more invested in their relationship, she might have been more apt to trust him.

God, he was sick of fruitless ifs. If Fluffy hadn't jumped on Judy's chest at the crucial moment, Judy might be with him now. They might be married, even planning a family.

And what would be wrong with that?

Aaron's eyes flew open with the realization. *Nothing, that's what.* When he put all the elements together, they sounded...wonderful. Not scary. Not repugnant. Not any of the things he would have expected them to be scarcely a month ago. And why was he surprised? He'd known from that moment of revelation in the science museum that he was in love with her. In love. The grown-up kind this time, for the first time. The kind that meant children and mortgages and till death do us part and maybe even a refrigerator with an ice dispenser in the door. The kind that meant a union of two lives for the enrichment of both. The kind that kept growing.

If Fluffy hadn't jumped on her chest at the crucial moment . . . Damn the fuzzy little bag of pedigreed bones!

Aaron hadn't heard his mother puttering in the kitchen or her footsteps as she approached, so he was surprised when she cleared her throat. He looked up to discover her standing just inside the den with a steaming mug in her hand. "You look as though you could use this," she said.

He took the mug she offered and grinned at her. "You're the only person I know who would bring hot chocolate with marshmallows in it to a thirty-two-year-old corporate vice president."

"I occasionally make hot chocolate with marshmallows in it for a fifty-nine-year-old orthopedic surgeon, despite cholesterol, calories and all the obnoxious things in chocolate." She smiled at him in a distinctively motherly way. "Like father, like son."

Aaron tested the temperature of the cocoa with the tip of his tongue and took a tentative sip. It was just hot enough, just chocolaty enough, made with whole milk and real cocoa rather than a mix.

"You were out walking a long time," his mother said, and when he didn't answer she asked, "Do you miss the snow already?"

"I just felt like a walk, that's all."

Maxine had sat down in the big recliner that was her husband's favorite chair. "Penny for your thoughts."

He grinned sheepishly. "I'm not sure you're prepared to hear what I was thinking when you came in."

"I'm game for the shock if you're game to talk." Again the only response she got was a wall of silence. She sighed and followed his gaze to the fire. The new log had caught and was burning evenly, and the flames danced beautifully along its length, a burnished brilliance that flickered in the near-darkness of the room.

He had not turned on the lights. That in itself was telling. He'd been moping around as though he'd come home for a funeral instead of for Christmas. "I know we haven't been . . . close in recent years," Maxine said, "but I'd listen and try to understand. An objective viewpoint helps sometimes."

He turned his head to watch her face. "If you must know, I was just regretting the fact that you're not going to be a grandmother."

Once, when he was eight years old, she'd discovered a dead field mouse when she was dropping a quarter in the pocket of his denim coveralls. The look she gave him now was similar to the one she'd given him then. "You were right, son. I wasn't prepared for that."

"You were always disappointed that you couldn't have more children, weren't you?"

Her eyes narrowed at the tincture of bitterness in his voice. "You say that as though I felt one wasn't enough. Sure, I would have loved to have had kids running all over the estate. And we were one of the lucky families who could have afforded it. But I was never disappointed in you. I wouldn't trade a dozen unknowns for the son I have."

"Even though I haven't given you the grandchildren you want?"

"Poor Jerry," she said, smiling sadly, "shouldering all the responsibility because you're the only one I can put the thumbscrews to. It's always been that way, hasn't it? I guess that's just another drawback of being the only child. Naturally I'm anxious for grandbabies. You can't blame me for being a little impatient. It's been thirty-two years since I've had a baby in the house."

She studied the flames dancing on the log pensively. "Getting old is scary, son. It tends to make a person search for some small measure of immortality. If we didn't feel a need to perpetuate ourselves, I'd bet the entire human race would fizzle out due to lack of interest, especially since science has given us birth control."

Aaron rapped a tit-a-tat, tit-a-tat rhythm on the side of the mug. Maxine waited for him to bring up what was on his mind, but he had retreated into a private world of thought. He'd been there too often of late. She could tell when her son was deeply troubled. Finally she said, "This talk about children—is it the product of a vague yearning, a feeling that life's passing you by, or is there a specific woman involved?''

He took a long draft of the warm chocolate, swallowed it and said flatly, "Oh, there's a woman.''

"In Florida?''

He nodded.

"Virginia's son's friend?''

Aaron scowled at her. "For two women who lost touch for over thirty years, you two certainly reestablished channels of communication in a hurry.''

"Virginia is very sorry that she put you in an embarrassing situation.''

"Embarrassing hardly covers the situation. The whole thing was asinine from beginning to end.''

"Virginia says she's a very nice girl, very smart. Level-headed.''

That at least got his attention. "Virginia's never met Judy.'' After a beat, he added uncertainly, "Has she?''

"Only on the phone. She called her to apologize for what she did and thank her for the advice she gave Gregory.''

"Which was?'' A muscle twitched in Aaron's jaw.

"She told him to make peace with his mother.''

"She what?'' he asked.

"She told him that although Virginia's methods were off-kilter, she had obviously acted out of concern, so he should make peace with her and not let misguided intentions destroy their relationship. So Gregory forgave her, and now Virginia's only dilemma is deciding what to do about the four hundred dollars he spent on the dog. This girl—''

"Judy,'' Aaron supplied.

Maxine raised her eyebrow at his defensive tone. "Judy, is it? Well, she volunteered to pay for the dog, but Virginia wouldn't hear of it. After all, it was Gregory who bought it."

"We could always strangle the dog," Aaron said under his breath.

"Please don't mumble, Jerry."

"I said—" he spoke with deliberate clarity "—I don't suppose it's occurred to Virginia that she could have Gregory work it off—mow the yard or clean the pool or something equally menial?"

Now Maxine grinned. "I'll mention it to her."

"Do me a favor and don't tell her where the idea came from."

A long silence ensued, a silence that lent itself to sipping cocoa and watching a fire. It ended when Aaron placed his cup on the lacquer coaster on the coffee table.

"Tell me about this girl," Maxine said.

"Her name is Judy Harte. She's a schoolteacher. I think . . . I have a feeling you'd like her."

"Are you in love with her?"

"Yes, but..." Aaron sighed wearily. "I think I'd like to talk about it. Maybe I *need* to talk about it. But I wouldn't want anything I said to get back to Virginia Simpson."

Maxine got up, walked to the sofa and sat down on the arm of it next to Aaron. Lifting his hair back, she kissed his forehead. "I may seem like an old gossip to you, but I would never betray a confidence. You've got a problem, and I'd like to help. A mother can't stop being a mother just because her child grows up."

He didn't intend to tell her everything, all the intimate details, but once he started the telling the story poured out. His mother listened quietly, and though she said nothing her gentle nods were reassuring.

"So you see," he concluded, "if not for that scruffy little mutt Gregory bought, Judy and I might have been together, and we might still be together and you might be getting a grandbaby to bounce on your lap."

Maxine smiled at him indulgently. "It seems to me you're pinning a lot of might-have-beens and might-bes on a dumb animal."

"Might-have-beens and might-bes are all I have left." He sighed morosely. "They're not very warm company at night."

Maxine reached out for his hand and patted it. "Sometimes—" she paused to search for the most tactful way to put what she had to put to him "—sometimes we fool ourselves. I mean, it's human nature to want what we can't have and devalue what's available."

"My track record on lasting relationships isn't very good, is it?"

Maxine refrained from further comment, and Aaron frowned. "This thing with Judy is different," he said. "It's . . . it's as though this is the first time I've ever really known a woman and everything started when I met her. The past is . . . well, it's past, and it has nothing to do with the way I feel about her."

"Do you think she loves you?"

"She *loved* me," he said. "She admitted it when she was so upset and angry. But as to how she feels about me now . . ." He shook his head. "They say it's a thin line between love and hate."

She patted his hand again. "They also say love conquers all."

"Judy may be the exception that defies that rule. I've done everything I can do to make her listen to reason, and she's still hopping mad. And hurt." He closed his eyes against the memory of Judy's tears. "God knows, I didn't mean to hurt her."

"Maybe after she's had some time to think about it, Judy will come to realize that."

"I wish I could believe that."

"Time has a way of working miracles we can only dream of," Maxine said.

"This miracle's going to take more than time if it happens at all." He slapped his knee with his hand. "Damn! It's so frustrating. I know if I could just get her alone somewhere and make her listen...but kidnapping was against the law the last time I checked."

Maxine rose from the arm of the chair and walked closer to the fire and stared at the flames. "There are degrees of kidnapping," she said.

Aaron cocked his head, wondering if he'd heard her correctly. "What are you thinking?"

She waved away the question. "Nothing. Just thinking aloud." After a long silence, she turned to her son. "How would you feel about a houseguest for a week or so?"

He chuckled. "You? Singular? Without Dad?"

"Virginia's been trying to get me to come for a few days so she and I can have a good old-fashioned gab session, and I can't think of a better time. Your father's going to be playing the invisible husband for the rest of the ski season, and you're down in the dumps, so the company would do you good, too."

"Just like that?" He snapped his fingers in the air.

She snapped her fingers back and smiled indulgently. "Just like that. I'll call the airline to see if there's room on the plane." She paused on her way out the door. "As badly as I want grandchildren, I never wanted them at the expense of your happiness, Aaron. I've always thought you'd be happier with a wife and family, but I never thought you should settle for the wrong woman, and I'm glad you didn't. If you've found the right woman, I sincerely hope things work out. For everybody.''

You're up to something, Aaron thought as he watched her retreat. *I just hope whatever it is doesn't backfire.*

One good deed blowing up in a man's face was enough for a lifetime.

"Va-va-va-voom! Judy. You look sensational! What a dress!''

"Where did you come up with an expression like va-va-va-voom?'' Judy said, laughing.

"I saw it in an old movie,'' Gregory said.

"Well thank you. That's the nicest compliment I've had all year.'' The dress in question was a slinky gold lamé, high-necked in front with a deep-plunging drape in back and a very straight skirt that melded to the generous curve of her hips in a flattering way. Virginia Simpson had said her annual New Year's Eve party was the perfect opportunity to wear a "flat-out sexy'' dress, and this was the "flat-out'' sexiest dress Judy owned.

Gregory's hands lingered on her shoulders as he draped her lace shawl over them. "I could forget to pick up my date, and you and I could—''

Deftly rolling her shoulders out of his grip, Judy said, "You wouldn't want to stand a girl up on New Year's Eve, would you?''

"For a woman like you?'' he asked, eyeing her appreciatively. "In a heartbeat.''

"Behave or I'll tell your mother,'' she teased in a sing-song voice. Later, as Gregory drove to his parents' house, she asked, "Who usually comes to your parents' New Year's party?''

"People they've known a long time. Neighbors. People from my dad's office,'' he answered. Then, after a beat of silence, he volunteered, "I don't know if Aaron will be there. Will it bother you if he is?"

"I'll survive." *I hope.*

"You really fell for him, didn't you?"

Ah, youth! Judy thought. Everything was so simple to a nineteen-year-old. Love, chemistry and respect could all be condensed into a simple phrase: you really fell for him.

"Sometimes I'm sorry I told you about the whole thing," Gregory said. "I feel like I've ruined your life."

She laughed. She had to. Crying on the way to a party made no sense. "Gregory, you didn't ruin my life. If I'm disappointed in Aaron, it's because of what he did, not because you told me about it."

"Somebody ought to beat the tar out of him."

"What purpose would that serve?"

"It would teach him a lesson."

She smiled at his naiveté. "I doubt that."

Arriving at the Simpson house, Judy and Gregory were approached by a maid who took their coats. Seeing them, Virginia welcomed them immediately.

"Judy," Virginia said, taking her hand as Gregory introduced them. "It's so nice to finally meet you in person." She eyed her from head to toe. "You're as pretty as Gregory said you are, and that's saying a lot."

"Mother!" Gregory interjected, his cheeks reddening.

"That's a splendid dress," Virginia said.

Judy looked at Virginia's black satin dress with its huge pink sash that ended in a tall ruffle that flounced over one shoulder. "Yours is rather splendid, too, Mrs. Simpson."

"Oh, thank you. I just love getting all dolled up for a party, don't you?" She folded her elbow and pulled Judy's hand through it, effectively guiding her away from Gregory. "Why don't I introduce you to the other guests while Gregory goes after his young lady."

Virginia was a gracious hostess, and Judy played the gracious guest, saying the proper phrases, smiling at the appropriate moments, listening attentively, making witty small talk. Yet she felt detached from the prevailing air of revelry, as though she were an observer instead of a participant. She was, she realized finally, in an agitated state of anticipation. Was Aaron going to be here or wasn't he?

Masochist! she told herself. *You're hoping he's here. And what are you going to do if he is? Have you thought about that?*

Absurd question! Of course she'd thought about it. Since accepting Virginia Simpson's invitation, the thought had been her constant companion—Aaron might be there.

Virginia's next-door neighbor Elizabeth, a slightly plump woman wearing a satin shirtwaist tunic over panne velvet slacks, was elaborating on the details of the outdoor cultivation of poinsettias when Judy first caught sight of Aaron at the wet bar, pouring wine into stemmed goblets. Her vantage point in the corner was fortunate. While she could see him, she was shielded from his sight by the fullness of Elizabeth's ample body. Her eyes followed his progress as he carried the two glasses of wine across the room and handed one to a woman she could see only from the back.

She had never considered that he might bring a date. In all the scenarios she'd imagined, her mind had never seen fit to supply him with a woman. She stared at the woman, who was tall and slender, with her fair hair sleekly upswept. Her clothes were understated and elegant, coupling the simplicity of a floor-length tapestry skirt with the extravagant frivolity of a pale pink Victorian blouse.

Judy felt as though a machete had just been embedded in her heart. Oh, God, why had she ever agreed to come and subject herself to this?

Because you thought you'd see him, he'd profess his undying love for you again and beg you for forgiveness and you'd forgive him and—

And what, you ninny? she chided herself.

And we'd glide into each other's arms and tread gently off to happily-ever-after land, she admitted to herself, fighting to control the quivering of her bottom lip and blink back the tears that were welling up inside her.

Fool! she thought. *Silly, romantic fool!* She was on the verge of losing the battle against tears when Elizabeth saved her by asking a question that required a specific reply. Focusing her attention on mundane garden talk did not assuage the pain knifing through Judy's heart, but as she talked the unshed tears subsided into a lump in her throat. Noticing her sudden hoarseness, Elizabeth's husband offered to mix her a drink, and Judy gratefully dispatched him to the bar for a refill of the house specialty, frozen piña coladas.

He returned with the drink and said, "Elizabeth, the Lowells are here. Ted insisted I bring you over to say hello. Won't you come with us, Judy?"

"Oh, yes," Elizabeth insisted, resting her hand on Judy's arm for emphasis. "You'll adore Scott and Dolly."

So Judy was forced to leave the sanctuary of the corner. Chancing a quick glance in the direction where she'd last seen Aaron, she was relieved to see that he and his date were no longer there. Still, she did her best to burrow into the cluster of people surrounding her as they walked.

If not for the inconvenience to Virginia Simpson, she would plead a headache and go home. Why in the world hadn't she brought her own car instead of letting Virginia insist that Gregory drive her? Now he was out at a different party with his date, and the two of them weren't due back at the Simpsons' until just before midnight, so Virginia would have to draft her husband or a guest to take her home if she insisted on leaving.

Face it, ninny, you're stuck for the duration, being a fifth wheel at the annual reunion of Elizabeth and Charlie and Scott and Dolly while you try to fake invisibility. Hip, hip, hooray and auld lang syne!

A voice from behind her cut through her self-absorbed musings. "Excuse me, but I couldn't help noticing your perfume." Judy turned and found herself nose-to-nose with the woman she'd seen with Aaron. It was a striking face she looked into, but not a young one. Twinkling blue eyes and great cheekbones did not disguise the fact that she was at least twenty years older than Aaron.

"My perfume?" Judy said limply.

"It smells suspiciously like an unopened Christmas package on the mantel in my son's living room. There's nothing sadder than an unopened package a week after Christmas, is there? They just sit there like an unfulfilled promise." She held out her hand. "I'm Maxine Aaron, an old sorority sister of Virginia's."

Maxine *Aaron*? "I'm Judy Harte," Judy said, shaking her hand.

"This particular package is especially sad," Maxine continued. "It's all lopsided and stained. To tell you the truth, it looks as though Jerry threw it across the room in a fit of anger or something."

"Jerry?" *Aaron's mother was in Connecticut, wasn't she?*

"My son—the one with the mangled package. I think something broke inside . . . because his entire condo smells like that perfume you're wearing. What did you say you called it?"

"Allure," Judy said softly.

"Allure. That's it. He at least told me the name of it, but that's all I can get out of him, except that he bought it for someone who wouldn't want it now and he didn't have the heart to return it to the store."

He'd bought her perfume! Judy felt the sting of tears she absolutely, positively could not shed.

"I tell you, that boy—a mother can call a son that even when he's thirty-two, can't she?—is acting positively daffy. You'd never even know he was here tonight the way he's been skulking around the fringe of the crowd as though he's hiding from someone. If I hadn't sent him for drinks occasionally, I don't think he would have spoken to a soul. I think this broken romance has unhinged him. He's been building something in his spare room, and I peeped at it this morning. It's a pinwheel, for Pete's sake."

"A pinwheel?" Judy asked incredulously.

"Incredible, isn't it? I wouldn't have believed it if I hadn't seen it myself. Jerry's not usually a putterer. But there it was, a six-foot-tall pinwheel."

Judy's cheeks were burning. Surely it was noticeable. "Mrs. Aaron, I'm sure your son wouldn't want you discussing..."

"His broken heart?" Maxine said. "Oh, I'm sure he wouldn't with a perfect stranger. It's unforgivable. But I don't have anyone else to talk it over with. My husband's back in Connecticut, my son won't discuss it, and Virginia—well, she just gets too guilt-ridden when I bring it up. You see, she prevailed upon Aaron to do a favor for her, and I think she used our friendship to get him to feel a sense of obligation to help her, and somehow that had something to do with this girl breaking up with Jerry."

"She pressured him because you and she..." Judy's voice was hoarse again.

Maxine nodded. "Aren't meddling old ladies a nuisance?"

"You and Virginia aren't..." She was about to say "old" when a noticeable wave of excitement passed through the crowd.

"It's almost midnight," Maxine said. "They're getting ready for the countdown. I promised Jere—my husband—that I would try to call at midnight, so I'd better get to the phone. Why don't you walk with me? That is, if there's no one you're planning on hugging at the turn of the year. It's going to be terribly loud and rowdy in here in a few minutes."

There was a note of authority in Maxine's voice that made what she said seem perfectly logical. Judy went with her to the hall telephone and stood a few feet away as Maxine dialed. Trace Simpson was passing out plastic champagne glasses, and Virginia was walking through the crowd with a box of shiny confetti, blowout whistles and colorful paper curls. Some shouted, "One minute," and the crowd began a sixty-second countdown, growing louder with each passing second. Judy was too preoccupied watching the merriment to notice Maxine gesturing an "okay" sign to Virginia and Virginia nodding back. Gregory had come in with his date. He spied Judy and waved. She waved back, only to have Trace press a champagne glass in her hand as she lowered it.

The countdown continued. "Ten, nine, eight...." Trace put down the glasses and worked a corkscrew into the cork of a bottle of champagne, then stood poised to press down the plungers of the corkscrew at the magic moment.

"Three, two, one...." The crowd went wild, tossing confetti, blowing the paper snakes, shouting, applauding the pop of the champagne cork. They paired off, hugging, kissing. Gregory kissed his date with an ardor that belied his earlier suggestion that he ditch her for an older woman. Maxine had her hand pressed to the ear that wasn't against the phone, trying to block out the noise. And Judy was alone in that noisy roomful of people, more alone than she'd ever been in her life.

In the confusion she didn't notice the movement behind her, and the arm that wrapped around her waist like a steel band caught her totally off guard. Her screams were lost in the general melee of celebration as she was lifted off the floor and carried backward through a door she'd scarcely noticed. She kicked, she punched at the arm holding her with balled fists, she screamed, all to no avail. Her abductor spun, closed the door behind them with his hips and leaned against it. One of his hands came up to cover her mouth and stifle her screams.

He said in her ear, "Don't bite, Judy. It's me," as he slowly lowered her feet to the floor and loosened his hold.

She spun around. "Aaron!"

"Happy New Year, sweetheart," he said as his mouth closed in on hers and his arms tightened around her again in a firm embrace. He kissed her artfully, urgently, thoroughly, nibbling at her lips until she parted them and then plundering her mouth with his tongue, tasting, devouring. She was weak when he lifted his mouth from hers and kissed his way across her cheek to the velvety skin of her neck.

"Do you know what you look like in that dress?" he whispered huskily. "It's taken every ounce of my self-control and some I didn't know I possessed to stay away from you."

"You've been watching me?"

"Ever since you came in." His breathing was heavy against her ear. "I've been going crazy without you." He kissed his way back to her mouth, and she slid her arms around his neck. With his arm supporting the small of her back, he lifted her literally off her feet as the kiss progressed from tender to tantalizing. When he finally eased her feet gently to the floor, she leaned against him for support and nestled her cheek against his chest. His fingertips stroked the soft skin of her back above the plunging drape of her dress. "I love you, Judy."

"I know," she said.

"You do?"

"Your mother told me."

"Mother *told* you? She was just supposed to find a way to get you near the door at midnight. I can do my own telling."

Judy lifted her cheek from his chest and looked at him. "You mean she knew who I was?"

"Of course."

"Everything she told me was meant for me," Judy mused aloud, a hint of wonderment in her voice. "All that chatter about the beat-up Christmas package and the pinwheel—are you really building a six-foot pinwheel?"

"The perfume broke," he said, slightly distracted. "Judy, my mother doesn't chatter. In thirty-two years, I've never heard her chatter."

"It was an act!" Judy said. "No wonder Virginia insisted I let Gregory drive. She didn't want to take any chances on my leaving."

"It appears we've been the target of some intrusive motherhood," Aaron said with a chuckle of consternation. "I don't know whether to strangle the both of them or kiss them."

She put her hand on his cheek and smiled. "For what it's worth, their little scheme worked. We're here, together."

A rowdy chorus of "Auld Lang Syne" filtered through the door. Aaron touched her cheek as she touched his. "It's a new year, Judy. A clean slate. Let's start that way, too. New, with nothing carried over except love. Oh, Judy, please tell me you love me. I need to hear it."

The seconds she hesitated were torturous to him.

"A scientist would say something very logical right now, like, 'You've told too many women you loved them and they've wound up hurt and I don't want to be next on your casualty list.'" For a moment, oh, so long a moment, she stared at him with large, limpid, serious eyes. "But I don't seem to have any scientific objectivity where you're concerned. All I can think of when you say you love me is that I don't want you to stop saying it, ever, and that I can't go on denying that I love you."

Her arms flew around his neck, and she planted kiss after kiss on his cheek, his forehead, his chin, and then hugged him. "Oh, Aaron, it feels so good not to fight it anymore."

"Marry me," he said, hugging her to him urgently. "For all the right reasons. Judy, I *want* to get married. I can hardly wait to get married. Let's say the vows and buy a house in the suburbs and have two point three babies."

She pulled away from him and tilted her head back so that she could see his face, and said firmly, "If it's all the same to you, I'd like to stop at two or go all the way to three. It's so hard trying to decide which thirty percent of a baby to get."

He laughed, a rich, resonant belly laugh composed of pure delight. "I'll never get tired of you."

"That's reassuring. Marriage and children are total commitments, and I'm not going to settle for a solo venture on child-rearing."

"No more solos," he said, "for either of us." He tweaked her nose with his thumb and forefinger. "Did you know I've been lying awake nights thinking about the babies we'd have, wondering what they'd look like and what it would feel like to hold them in my arms. Can we have one right away?"

She shook her head at his childlike exuberance and cradled his face in her hands. "It takes a minimum of nine months under the best of circumstances. Anyway, you're putting the cart before the horse. One thing at a time."

"Oh, yes," he said, as though he'd just remembered he was supposed to bring home a loaf of bread and a gallon of milk on the way home from the office. He reached into the inside breast pocket of his coat, pulled out a velvet jewelry case and flipped it open. "This is a bit unconventional, but it reminded me so much of you that I . . ."

It was a ring with oblong emeralds and sapphires set around a modest round-cut diamond. "It looks like a pinwheel," she said, flabbergasted.

"We could exchange it for something more—"

"Never!" she said. "Oh, Aaron, it's beautiful. It's the only ring I'd ever want now that I've seen it."

He slipped it on her finger, then raised her hand to his mouth and kissed it. "And you're the only woman I'll ever want. Now why don't you kiss me again before we go make my meddlesome mother the happiest woman in the world."

"The second happiest," Judy corrected as her arms went around him, and she stood on tiptoe so she could do as he asked.

*   *   *   *   *

Silhouette Romance

COMING NEXT MONTH

#544 THAT'S WHAT FRIENDS ARE FOR—Annette Broadrick
Brad Crawford had once loved Penny Blackwell so much he'd been
willing to let her go. But now Brad was back and determined to save
Penny from marrying the wrong man. After all, to love, cherish and
protect—isn't that what friends are for?

#545 KANE AND MABEL—Sharon De Vita
Kati Ryan's diner was her pride and joy, so sparks flew when Lucas
Kane showed up, claiming to be her new partner. Luke needed a
change of scenery and Kati fit the bill—he'd show her they were both
born to raise Kane.

#546 DEAR CORRIE—Joan Smith
When it came to Bryan Holmes, columnist Corrie James knew she
should take her own advice—"no commitment, no dice." But this
romantic playboy was simply too sexy to resist!

#547 DREAMS ARE FOREVER—Joyce Higgins
Cade Barrett was investigating Leigh Meyers's company for
investment purposes, but in her he found a more valuable asset. He
wanted her for his own, but she'd given up on childhood dreams of
happy endings. He'd have to prove that dreams are forever....

#548 MID-AIR—Lynnette Morland
Whenever Lorelei Chant worked with pilot-producer Chris Jansen,
his sky-blue eyes made her heart soar. The trouble was, Chris seemed
to like flying alone. Could Lorelei convince him that love can happen
in the strangest places—even in mid-air?

#549 TOUCHED BY MAGIC—Frances Lloyd
Architect Alexandra Vickery's new client, Lucien Duclos, was quite a
handful—arrestingly attractive and extremely suspicious of women
designers. Alex was determined to prove herself, but how could she
keep her composure when she discovered he was as attracted to her as
she was to him?

AVAILABLE THIS MONTH:

**#538 TREADMILLS AND
PINWHEELS**
Glenda Sands
#539 MAIL-ORDER BRIDE
Debbie Macomber
#540 CUPID'S ERROR
Brenda Trent

#541 A TENDER TRAIL
Moyra Tarling
**#542 COMPLIMENTS OF THE
GROOM**
Kasey Michaels
#543 MADELINE'S SONG
Stella Bagwell